YASUNARI KAWABATA

The Rainbow

Yasunari Kawabata, winner of the 1968 Nobel Prize in Literature, was one of Japan's most distinguished novelists. Born in Osaka in 1899, he published his first stories while he was still in high school. He graduated from Tokyo Imperial University in 1924. His story "The Izu Dancer," first published in 1926, appeared in *The Atlantic Monthly* in 1955. Among his major novels published in the United States are *Snow Country* (1956), *Thousand Cranes* (1958), *The Sound of the Mountain* (1970), *The Master of Go* (1972), and *Beauty and Sadness* (1975).

INTERNATIONAL

Also by Yasunari Kawabata

Snow Country

Thousand Cranes

The Sound of the Mountain

The Master of Go

Beauty and Sadness

House of the Sleeping Beauties and Other Stories

The Rainbow

The Rainbow

YASUNARI KAWABATA

Translated from the Japanese by Haydn Trowell

Vintage International
VINTAGE BOOKS
A DIVISION OF PENGUIN RANDOM HOUSE LLC
NEW YORK

A VINTAGE INTERNATIONAL ORIGINAL 2023

English-language translation copyright © 2023 by Haydn Trowell

All rights reserved. Published in the United States
by Vintage Books, a division of Penguin Random House LLC,
New York, and distributed in Canada by Penguin Random
House Canada Limited, Toronto. Originally published in Japan
as *Niji Ikutabi* in *Fujin Seikatsu,* serialized from 1950 to 1951 and
subsequently collected in *The Complete Works of Yasunari Kawabata*
(Vol. 12) published by Shinchosha, Tokyo, in 1951.
Copyright © 1950, 1951 by The Heirs of Yasunari Kawabata.

The Cataloging-in-Publication Data is available at the
Library of Congress.

Vintage International Trade Paperback ISBN: 978-0-593-31492-0
eBook ISBN: 978-0-593-31491-3

Book design by Nicholas Alguire

vintagebooks.com

Printed in the United States of America
10 9 8 7 6 5 4 3 2 1

Contents

The Rainbow

The Winter Rainbow

I

Asako saw a rainbow appear over the far shore of Lake Biwa.

The train had passed Hikone and was approaching Maibara. With it being the year-end holiday, the carriage was almost empty.

When had the rainbow appeared? It seemed as though, all of a sudden, it had floated to the surface of the lake that she had been watching through the window.

The man sitting in front of her had seen the rainbow too. "Chiiko, Chiiko, a rainbow, a rainbow, look, a rainbow has come out," he said, holding a baby up to the glass.

The two of them, Asako and the man, had been sitting across from one another in the four-seat compartment since the train had left Kyōto. Although, as the man was traveling with the child, there were really three of them.

Asako was sitting by the window. The man had taken the

seat by the aisle, but after the train passed through the tunnel at Higashiyama, he laid the baby down on the seat next to him, resting her head on his lap.

"A little high . . ." he murmured, and began to fold up his overcoat.

Her curiosity piqued, Asako watched as the man folded it into a small pillow and moved the baby down so that her head rested on his knees.

The baby, wrapped in a soft blanket decorated with a floral design, looked up at her father as she waved her arms.

Asako had guessed that the man was traveling alone with the child when she first glimpsed him on the platform. When he sat in the seat across from her, she had wondered whether she should offer to help in some way.

Holding the baby up to the window again, the man glanced toward her. "It's quite unusual to see a rainbow in winter, you know."

"Really?" Taken by surprise at being addressed all of a sudden, Asako found herself at a loss for words.

"No, that isn't right," the man contradicted himself. "It isn't all that unusual. We're already close to Maibara, and the Hokuriku Line from Maibara . . . well, when I was going from Kanazawa to Maibara on the way to Kyōto, there were lots of rainbows, unlike today. You can see lots of rainbows on the Hokuriku Line, you know, lots of pretty little rainbows. It must have been three or four years ago, but I can't remember the exact month. Anyway, when the train came out of a tunnel, you could see the sea, and there were rainbows rising over the hills all the way to the shore. There was some light snowfall in Kanazawa, so it must have been winter."

Had the man been traveling with the baby then too? So

Asako wondered, before realizing that the child wouldn't have been born three or four years ago. Laughing at herself, she said, "Whenever I see a rainbow, it makes me think of spring or summer."

"Yes, those colors aren't very winter-like, are they?"

"Are you going to Kanazawa?"

"Today?"

Asako nodded.

"We're going home to Tōkyō."

The baby pressed against the window with both hands.

"Does she know it's a rainbow?" Asako asked. She had been pondering the question for some time.

"Hmm . . ." The man paused in thought. "I suppose not. No, she probably doesn't."

"But she can see it, can't she?"

"She must be able to. But babies don't really look at distant things or have much interest in them. They don't need to. She probably isn't old enough to have a sense of distance, or of time either, for that matter."

"How old is she?"

"Nine months," the man said proudly before turning the baby around to face him. "I mustn't show you any more rainbows, Chiiko. I've been scolded by the young lady."

"Oh! I didn't mean . . . I just thought how happy she must be, to be on a train with her father at such a young age and to be shown a rainbow."

"She won't remember it."

"But if *you* remember, it will be a wonderful thing to tell her about when she's older."

"It will, won't it? When she gets older, she'll no doubt have to travel along the Tōkaidō herself from time to time."

The baby looked toward Asako, smiling.

"Then again, no matter how many times she might come back this way, who can say whether she'll ever see another rainbow rising over Lake Biwa? Miss, earlier you said she must be happy. I think for us adults, seeing such a large rainbow at the end of the year is a sign of happiness and of a good new year to come."

Asako was of the same opinion.

Since first catching sight of the rainbow on the far shore of the lake, she had felt as though it were calling out to her. She was filled with a strange yearning to go to that country beyond the rainbow while still alive; or more realistically, to visit its shores. She often journeyed along this route, but not once had she thought about the far shore of the lake. Indeed, of all the travelers who took the Tōkaidō Main Line, only a small number ever went there.

As the rainbow arced to the right, it seemed to Asako as though the train was heading toward the other side.

"The banks of the lake are covered with rapeseed and milk vetch fields," the man said. "In spring, when the flowers come out, seeing a rainbow rising over those fields must be happiness itself, wouldn't you say?"

"It does sound quite wonderful," Asako agreed.

"But seeing a rainbow in winter is a little strange, don't you think? It's like seeing a tropical flower blooming in the snow, or laying eyes on the lover of a deposed king. Maybe it's because the rainbow is cut off without forming a complete arc."

Just as the man had said, the rainbow was incomplete, disappearing into the heavy clouds.

Stagnant clouds that foretold snow hung low over the surface of the lake. Though they seemed to extend across the entirety of the surface, there must have been a gap some-where out of sight, as the far shore remained lit by a brilliant band of light. In front of the rainbow, soft beams of sunlight were glistening over the water.

The rainbow rose only as high as that band of light.

It looked as if it were climbing almost directly up into the sky. Perhaps because only its base could be seen, the rainbow seemed all the wider. To trace an arc, it would have to be truly gigantic, ending very far away indeed. But of course, only the base of the one side was visible.

On closer inspection, though, Asako realized that the rainbow didn't have a base at all. Rather, it looked as though it were floating in midair. It half seemed as though it were rising out of the water, and half as though it were rising from the ground of the far shore. As she followed its arc upward, it wasn't clear whether it disappeared into the clouds or before reaching them.

The rainbow appeared all the more vivid for its being cut so short. It seemed to call out to the clouds with a sense of sorrow as it ascended into the heavens. The more she looked at it, the more strongly she was taken by the feeling.

The clouds were of the thick, leaden kind, reaching down to the far shore like dark splotches of ink hanging motionless over the horizon.

The rainbow disappeared from sight before the train reached Maibara.

The man brought a trunk down from the overhead lug-gage rack.

It seemed to be filled only with things for the baby. There was a neat pile of diapers and a peach-colored change of clothes tucked into one corner.

It looked like he was about to change the baby's diaper.

"Shall I . . . ?" Asako began, leaning forward, but stopped. She had meant to ask whether she should help, but the words sounded strange to her, and died in her mouth.

"Don't worry, miss," the man said, without meeting her gaze. "I'm used to doing it."

He laid a sheet of newspaper over the seat, upon which he set a fresh diaper.

"My!" Asako looked on in admiration.

"See? I know what I'm doing," the man said with a laugh. "How about you?"

"Not really, but I was taught how to do it at school."

"At school? Well, I guess there's that."

"I *can* do it. I've watched others, and I'm a woman, after all."

"I suppose so. I've been doing this so long I'm starting to get sick of it."

Asako saw the name Ōtani written on a tag attached to the man's trunk. The luggage was divided into three compartments. The section at the side was for the milk bottles, the center contained fresh diapers and a change of clothes, and tucked into the far edge was a vinyl bag.

Ōtani did indeed seem to know what he was doing. He wiped between the girl's legs three or four times. The skin was slightly reddened. Asako looked away. Ōtani folded the used diaper into a ball and deftly settled the baby into a new one before fastening its button.

"Well, would you look at that?" exclaimed a man from across the aisle. The whole carriage seemed to be looking in their direction.

Ōtani wrapped the baby in the blanket, put the soiled

diaper into a vinyl bag, and took what looked like a large vanity case from the corner of the trunk. Inside was a tin box, and inside the tin box were a thermos and a milk bottle with measurements.

Asako was overcome with emotion; but the longer she watched, the more her admiration began to turn into something approaching pity.

Even so, she smiled as she watched the baby drink from the bottle.

"I'm sorry you had to see that," Ōtani said.

Asako shook her head firmly. "Not at all. I thought you did a fine job."

"Her mother is in Kyōto, you see."

"Oh."

Was he separated from the baby's mother? But she couldn't ask such a thing.

Ōtani looked to be in his early thirties, with bushy eyebrows and a face that, even clean-shaven, hinted at a thick beard, giving the impression of a slight pallor that spread from his forehead to close to his ears. He had an altogether tidy appearance.

Black hairs could be seen on the fingers of the hand that held the baby.

When the child had finished drinking the milk, Asako held out a candied plum.

"Is it all right to give her this?" she asked, showing it to Ōtani.

"Of course," he replied, taking the sweet and placing it in the baby's mouth. "A thousand-year pebble," he murmured.

"Yes, like in the national anthem. I'm sure she'll grow up to be a wonderful lady."

Asako watched for the baby's cheeks to swell. When they didn't, she was struck by a sudden dread that the child might have swallowed the sweet whole, but she was soon able to breathe a sigh of relief.

2

"A happy new year to you," Ōtani said to Asako when they stepped off the train at Tōkyō Station.

It was a typical parting phrase for the turn of the year, but his words carried a particular warmth.

"Thank you. A happy new year to you as well, and to the baby too," Asako replied.

As she spoke, the rainbow over Lake Biwa floated up before her.

Naturally, it was but a brief farewell between strangers.

Returning home, Asako greeted her elder sister before asking, "Is Father in?"

"No," Momoko snapped.

"Oh?"

"Isn't that obvious?"

Asako slumped down to warm herself by the hibachi brazier. As she unfastened the buttons of her overcoat, she glanced toward Momoko. "Are you going out too?"

"Yes."

"Oh." She rose with a start and headed for the corridor.

"He's out," her sister's shrill voice pursued her. "There's no need to pry into his room."

"Yes, but . . ." she whispered, so quietly that her sister couldn't have heard.

She slid open the shōji screen to let some light into her father's room. "White camellias," she murmured when she saw the flowers arranged in a rustic Iga vase in the tokonoma alcove.

As she approached, she noticed that the hanging scroll by the vase was the same one that had been on display before she left for Kyōto. Only the flowers were changed.

She glanced over her father's desk for a moment before turning to leave. The empty space had a certain loneliness about it, but at the same time, Asako found it somehow comforting.

Back in the living room, the maid had already cleared the table.

It looked like her sister had eaten alone.

Momoko looked up at Asako. "So have you checked his room?"

"I wasn't *checking* it."

"It must feel uncomfortable, coming home from your trip to an empty house," Momoko said gently. "You should go get changed. The bath is ready."

"Yes."

"How listless you look! Are you tired?"

"No, it was a nice trip. The train was almost empty."

"Come, sit down." Momoko laughed, offering her some tea. "If you were coming back today, why didn't you send us a telegram? If you had let us know, Father might have stayed home."

Asako sat in silence.

"He left at around four o'clock. He's been late coming home recently."

"Oh, Momoko!" Asako exclaimed. "You're wearing your hair up! Show me!"

"No, no!" her sister protested, hiding the nape of her neck with her hands.

"Please, let me see."

"No, I won't."

"Why not? When did you change it? Please, turn that way, let me see." Asako knelt at her sister's back and rested a hand on her shoulder.

"No, you're embarrassing me."

Momoko was blushing all the way down to her neck. Perhaps realizing that her protestations must have seemed excessive, she resigned herself to silence.

"My hairline is too high. It looks strange, doesn't it?"

"Not at all. It suits you. You look wonderful."

"As if *I* could ever look wonderful," Momoko said, her shoulders stiffening.

The boy, her lover, always lifted her hair to kiss the nape of her neck. She had put it up to make it easier for him. He must have picked up the habit from her, after she had started kissing him that way too.

But Asako couldn't have known that this was the reason for her sister's self-conscious modesty.

It was rare for Asako to see the nape of her sister's neck. Momoko's hairline was indeed high, but that only gave it an added freshness and made her neck look longer and thinner. The hollow in the middle of the nape was deeper than average, accentuating her faint shadow.

Asako began to arrange some stray hairs, her fingers brushing against her sister's skin.

"Oh!" Momoko exclaimed, shivering. "So cold! Too cold!"

She was trembling, just as she did when the boy's lips rested on that spot.

Surprised, Asako withdrew her hand.

Momoko hesitated, afraid of accidentally revealing the secret behind her new hairstyle. With her sister at home, it had become suddenly difficult for her to leave for her rendezvous.

Her emotions getting the better of her, Momoko's voice turned brash. "Asako. Now that you're back from Kyōto, there's something you want to ask Father, isn't there?" she asked, turning around. "I know. There's no need to hide it. It was a lie, wasn't it, when you said you were going to see a newly married friend?"

"It wasn't a lie."

"Oh? So it wasn't a lie. You went to see your friend, but that wasn't your main reason for going, was it?"

Asako hung her head.

"Why don't you tell me?" Momoko paused, softening her tone. "And did you find this younger sister of ours in Kyōto?"

Asako stared back, taken by surprise.

"Did you?"

She shook her head slightly.

"You didn't?"

Asako nodded.

"Oh? I see." Momoko, until now staring at her sister so intently, looked away. "That's for the best." She all but spat out the words.

"Momoko!" Asako exclaimed, tears welling in her eyes. "What is it?"

"Father doesn't know, does he? That I went to look for her?"

"I couldn't say."

"But he can't!"

"Who knows? He's very perceptive, and if even I could figure it out . . ."

"Momoko, have you said something to him?"

"As if I would have! What a foolish girl you are!" Momoko brought her gaze back to meet Asako's. "Don't cry. There's no need to cry."

"But I thought it best not to say anything. Should I have told him? I should have told you at least."

"It doesn't really matter. The important thing is whether you should have gone looking for this sister of ours in the first place, don't you think?"

Asako stared back in silence.

"Why *did* you go? For Father's sake? For ours? For your mother? For our other sister?"

"It wasn't for anyone's sake."

"Then maybe you feel some sense of responsibility?"

Asako shook her head.

"Fine. Then let's say it was sentimentality. You went looking for her because you feel a sense of affection for her. Whether you find her or not, whether you communicate it or not, what really matters, both for you and for her, is that the affection is there. And if one day you do happen to meet her, that affection will flower again. That's what I think."

"Momoko . . ."

"Let me finish. But everyone has their own way of swimming, and everyone has a current suited to their own nature.

She's a Kyōto girl. How do you think she would have reacted to an outsider showing up in her life all of a sudden? It's like they say, from siblings come strangers. Let her live as she likes. You should think about what you're doing."

"But what will Father think?"

"Who knows? You know the saying, that you can't know the depths of a person's heart, the depths of the time they've lived. There are parts to Father even you don't understand."

"Doesn't *he* talk like that every now and then?"

"Yes. Whenever he wants to escape from an awkward situation." Momoko chuckled. "Whether it's someone's past or future, it's all to be found in the depths of their heart and the time they've lived."

Asako nodded.

Momoko looked toward her, as though to gauge her expression. "Before your mother died, she was quite worried about our sister in Kyōto. That's why you went looking for her, isn't it?"

The accusation had hit the mark.

"But you can't know what your mother was really thinking. She was so kind that she probably thought of the Kyōto girl as her own, even though she was born to another woman. Maybe she even believed she could come and live with us here. We had better assume she forgave everything before she passed away; otherwise, what you've done would be too cruel to her memory. But you can't know for sure what she was thinking. What a fool you were to go to Kyōto, thinking you were doing well by her!"

Asako hid her face in her hands and began to sob.

"Well, that's that. I'm going out."

Asako's shoulders were trembling.

"Won't you stop? If you keep on crying like that, I won't be able to leave."

"Momoko . . ."

"I'm sorry about this, but I have to go. Go take a bath. I'll leave then, okay?"

"Y-yes." Sobbing, Asako stumbled out of the sitting room. She clung to the edge of the bathtub, crying.

The sound of Momoko leaving through the front door echoed throughout the house.

Asako's tears began to well anew.

All of a sudden, she remembered a passage from her mother's diary.

Your mother, Momoko had said, because although they shared a father, they had been born to two different women.

Momoko has been cavorting with one boy after another. Maybe her bad experience with the first boy she loved is to blame? Or maybe it's because she indulged herself with other girls at school? Maybe she suffers from a lack of femininity?

Asako's mother had written that both she and her father had had their doubts, that neither knew the truth of the situation.

Her mother had written down something that her father had said, perhaps jokingly: *The world has become an easy place for seducing pretty young men.*

One after another was probably an exaggeration, but Asako herself had seen her sister in the company of no fewer than three young men.

The fear and shame evoked by that diary entry brought an end to her tears.

Traces of Dreams

I

Since the end of the war, countless villas in the resort town of Atami—the properties of former princes, of former nobles, and of former industrialists—had been transformed into inns and hotels.

The Camellia House was one such villa, having belonged to a former prince who had held the honorary title of Fleet Admiral.

Asako's father, Mizuhara Tsuneo, pointed out the window of the car as they passed by the entrance. "Do you see those two villas? They don't really look like inns, do they? That one belonged to a prince, and the one over there belonged to a marquis. The marquis was descended from royalty, but I heard he was wounded during the war. His leg, you see. Now they say he's been sentenced to forced labor as a war criminal."

They stepped out of the car by the gate to the Camellia House.

Mizuhara paused for a moment, looking around. "I used to walk this path often, a long time ago now, trying to sneak a glimpse of the prince. But I could never go inside. The gate was always locked."

The road led to Kinomiya and a plum orchard, and farther on, to Jikkoku Pass.

The hills on the right were fading into dusk. A white haze was rising from amid the darkened pines. In the dim light, the steam from the hot springs seemed to be meandering around the trees as though a thing alive.

"On that hill over there is the villa that belonged to the head family of the Fujishima conglomerate. You wouldn't know it was there from the road, would you? It was built nestled into the hill, to completely hide it from all angles," Mizuhara said. "They say you have to go through a tunnel just to get inside, and at the end of the tunnel, there's a thick iron door. They must have been afraid of unrest during the war."

The road seemed to pass through the hill, on the slopes of which stood the Camellia House. From below, it looked to be only two stories high; but once they entered the garden, they could see that it was actually three.

"We've reserved the cottage for you," the porter said, guiding them along a paved path through the garden to a detached building. "I hope you'll find it to your liking."

"What kind of flower is that?" Asako asked as she came to a stop by a tree.

"It must be a cherry blossom," the porter answered.

"A cherry blossom? But it doesn't look like a winter cherry."

"The winter cherries bloomed around the end of January. They've already lost their flowers."

"What do you think, Father?"

Mizuhara had been lost in thought ever since she first mentioned it. "What indeed? I can't quite remember the name. But it must be some sort of winter cherry."

"The leaves come out first on that one, the flowers second," the porter told them. "The flowers bloom facing downward, like they're wilting."

"Really? It looks a little like a crab apple."

As Asako had observed, the flowers were tinged scarlet. They were grouped together tenderly, sprouting from amid the leaves, just like a crab apple.

There was something indescribably dear about the pale green leaves scattered among the flowers in the late-February evening mist.

"Oh!" Asako exclaimed. "There are ducks in the pond!"

"I remember seeing Mexican ducks in the pond of Marquis Iga's residence next door," her father observed. "I wonder what happened to them."

Cherry blossoms were flowering on the other side of the pond.

As though floating in the middle of the water stood another detached building, a tearoom. The porter explained that it was built by the industrialist Narita, a former baron.

"I'd like to take a look at it, if there are no·guests staying at the moment," Mizuhara said.

As an architect, he had taken an ineffable interest in seeing how the houses of former nobles were being transformed into inns and restaurants.

Even the former residence of the emperor's younger

brother in Zushi had been turned into an inn. So too had the Odawara villa of the late Yamagata Aritomo. Such cases were too numerous to count.

However, the buildings had originally been designed as private residences and were ill-suited for their new roles, so Mizuhara was often invited to discuss remodeling them.

Even though the Camellia House, which included the main building, the cottage, and the tearoom, could accommodate only eight groups of guests, it had a spacious garden.

The cottage seemed most unusual to Asako as a guest room at a hot spring inn.

"How relaxing. It's like a farmhouse, so quiet and intimate."

"Indeed. This kind of simplicity is rather nice."

The building had been dismantled, transported from its original location, and rebuilt with care; but one would hardly have been able to tell.

"It's so natural and peaceful." Asako glanced around the room. "Oh! There's no transom window."

The room, eight tatami mats in size, was divided from the adjoining six-mat room by a wooden partition fitted with shōji screens two feet in height. The screens on the southern wall, and those on part of the western one, came only to waist height and weren't fitted with glass. The wood, both on the screens and on the ceiling, was uniformly dark and sooty. Though fitted with bright lightbulbs, the room nonetheless seemed dim, no doubt due to the color of the wood. Only the wood of the tokonoma alcove was of a different color. Even the texture of the tatami mats was rougher than usual.

No sooner had Mizuhara changed into a padded kimono than he went out into the garden to have a look at the tearoom. Asako had had no time to change.

In the six-mat pavilion, there was a four-and-a-half-mat room used for the tea ceremony, and a smaller one that looked more like a kitchen or a bathroom than a typical preparation area.

"One could practically live here," Mizuhara said, stepping out onto the bridge and looking up at the main building, designed in a Western style.

The house and the garden weren't worth the effort that he had once expended trying to catch a glimpse of them as a young man.

In a corner of the lawn at the bottom of the garden was a kennel, beside which a large dog was resting.

"What a fine Akita," Mizuhara said before approaching and petting the animal on the head.

As though by habit, the dog reared up onto its hind legs and rested its front paws on Mizuhara's waist. It had a thin coat of a light yellowish color, but the fur at its ears and wagging tail approached a tawny hue. Mizuhara rubbed the back of its head and hugged its plump neck. An impression of vivid beauty flowed into his chest.

He wanted to tell his daughter how the town of Atami, with its haphazardly constructed, dilapidated buildings, paled in comparison to the beauty of the dog.

But Asako wasn't paying attention. "Look at the daphne! It's already flowering! Ah, it smells just like spring!" She spoke as though it were the scent of happiness itself. "And the nandina under the scarlet-blossomed plum is coming into leaf. See? The leaves are red! But the tree is flowering late for a scarlet-blossomed plum, don't you think?"

"It is, isn't it? The white-blossomed plums have mostly lost their flowers by now."

"It really is a scarlet-blossomed plum, almost a deep carmine."

Mizuhara had learned from observing his wife that a short journey with the promise of release from one's domestic captivity could brighten a woman's spirits, especially when traveling with family. So too seemed to be the case for his daughter.

Asako found a lemon hanging from the branch of a small tree. "How pretty!" she whispered as she took hold of it gently. There was just the one fruit, small and still green.

"When I visited the garden of the villa next door, Marquis Iga's residence, the mimosas were all in bloom. What time of year could it have been? Well, when I entered the garden, there were some white peacocks roaming the lawn, and there were two or three Mexican ducks at the edge of the pond. The ducks seemed to be cold and didn't look to be doing too well, so it must have been winter. I say *pond*, but it was more like an open-air bath or a hot spring. The marquis was keeping angelfish in it. Tropical fish were so popular back then. All the stores were selling them. The marquis was trying to keep them in the thermal waters, you see. They grew so big. It was quite a success. Mimosas might not be so uncommon these days, but I saw them for the first time in that garden. It was a kind of hobby, I suppose. All sorts of small tropical birds were flitting about by that spacious hot spring."

"My!"

"The tropics were his hobby. The ground around the washing area was laid with stones from the Amazon. He had them brought all that way." As he spoke, Mizuhara began to walk toward the villa.

"The Amazon?" Asako seemed puzzled.

"A river in Brazil. They were red stones. They must have been covered with the droppings of those tropical birds, being so close to the water. And there were all these vivid tropical plants near the wall by the side of the hot spring. There must have been flowers too. There was an opaque glass window that stretched from the top of the wall to the bottom, opening onto the garden. It shone so glaringly bright. It was the kind of thing that makes us timid, formal Japanese feel ill at ease. It was like being in the tropics, what with all those bright colors. And inside, there was a high-ceilinged hall. And so many chairs. Well, the guests could exercise naked, or lie sprawled about if they wanted, or even enjoy themselves in the hot spring. Quite different from sitting modestly with only one's head poking out above the water, wouldn't you say?"

The white villa to the right of the Camellia House stood out against the last glimmers of dusk.

"It used to be even more vividly white. During the bombings, they used to say it would make an easy target, what with you being able to see it from so far away. But in any event, its design just goes to show how arrogant the marquis was. He must have been a little tyrant. It used to be a traditional garden, but they say that when he came back from the West, he had all the trees uprooted, all the rocks dug out, just so he could turn it into a lawn. It might not have been the most elegant arrangement, but it wouldn't have deserved to be turned into a Western-style park like this. But the marquis wanted to live in Atami as if it were the tropics. He kept the temperature inside at a constant seventy degrees all year round by running the water from the hot spring under the floor and through the walls, which ended up causing them

to crack. They hadn't researched the building materials well
enough, I suppose. When I visited, it was sweltering hot.
Very unpleasant."

"Seventy degrees?"

"Well, around that, I think. They say that even in the
middle of winter, the marquis would dictate to his typist wearing nothing thicker than a shirt. The typist was a
second-generation Japanese American he brought back from
overseas. The marquis would dictate his essays in English to
be published in foreign journals."

"My! Was he a scholar?"

"A zoologist. He would go on hunting expeditions to the
tropics. He apparently even visited Egypt by airplane. He
was more at home overseas, and more well-known too. I suppose he was the kind of man who found it difficult to live in
our cramped, gloomy Japan. So he shut himself away in this
tropical house, so at odds with its environment." Mizuhara
stopped. "It's no wonder it's falling apart."

He lifted his gaze toward a spire-like room jutting forth
from the roof.

"There was a hummingbird here when I visited. There
were two originally, but one of them died."

"Those little birds that fly so fast you can hardly see them?"

"Yes."

The lights came on in the Camellia House, illuminating
the garden from above.

Mizuhara took this as an opportunity to retrace his steps.

"I even got to see the upstairs bedroom. I was surprised,
of course, by the beautiful bed, and the assorted perfumes
and creams; but most shocking of all were the shoes. Behind
the curtain by the bed, there was shelf after shelf contain-

ing maybe fifty pairs of shoes, all belonging to the marquis's wife. She too was a second-generation Japanese American brought up overseas, so she was probably used to that way of life. The bedroom, just like the bathroom, wasn't the kind of thing you would think to find belonging to a Japanese. There was a large crescent-shaped window, fitted with a single pane of glass. It really was quite bright, quite florid."

He paused, then began talking about the American-style kitchen and bathroom.

They crossed the small bridge in front of the tearoom, when he let out a quiet chuckle. "Ah, now I remember. That tree we saw earlier, it's called a *scarlet winter cherry*!"

2

"Shall I wash your back?" Asako asked as she cleaned her own chest. "How long has it been since I washed your back last?"

Her father, immersed in the bathtub, rested his head on the edge. "Hmm. When you were little, I used to wash you all the way down to the gaps between your toes. Do you remember?"

"I wasn't such a child."

Mizuhara closed his eyes. "I've been thinking of having a house built for you."

"Oh? A house for me?"

"Yes."

"But who should I live with? Not by myself?" Asako spoke lightheartedly as she washed herself.

Though her questions had torn him from his thoughts, Mizuhara asked teasingly, "There isn't anyone who comes to mind?"

"No!" Asako turned suddenly to her father.

"Well, it would be fine even if it were just you. You wouldn't even have to live in it. It would be enough for me just to leave it to you. I'm an architect, after all. Isn't it natural for me to want to leave a small property to each of my daughters?"

"*Leave?*" Asako repeated dubiously before shaking her head with a shudder. "What a horrible thought!" She stepped into the bathtub. "It's gotten cold."

"I didn't mean anything like that. Like I've always said, there are all manner of unsatisfactory things in this world, but there's no art more subject to constraints than architecture. On top of the location, the materials, the purpose, the size, the budget, and the client's own demands, you have the carpenters, the painters, and the furniture makers too to take into account. Unlike Marquis Iga, I don't think I've ever been able to build a house to my own tastes. What I meant was a house built entirely to my own design. It would be my first time ever actually being able to do it." He spoke as though to erase all memory of the word *leave,* but there remained a hint of sadness to his voice.

Mizuhara found himself startled by his daughter's natural beauty.

He suddenly remembered the sight of the Akita that he had seen in the garden. It was wrong, he knew, to compare his daughter to a dog, but both were beautiful in their own distinct ways. Of course, it was quite impossible to compare those two kinds of beauty.

The dog had been tied to a kennel. Mizuhara considered

the nests and burrows of animals, who were unable to build houses, to be more respectful to nature than human architecture. Even if they damaged the surrounding landscape, they weren't ugly. He thought of Atami as an example of the squalor to which architecture reduced the environment. He could see no way of saving it. In much the same way as the advances of science had created new miseries for mankind, he doubted that modern architecture would be able to increase people's overall happiness. Such doubts weren't unusual for him.

Moreover, as with many architects around the world, he had his doubts that modern architecture, compared to that of the past, would endure as a testament to beauty.

Struck by his daughter's pristine beauty, he found himself doubting whether he truly possessed the skill and ability to design for her an appropriately beautiful house. And that sense of doubt startled him all the more.

It was as though he had forgotten the beauty and love that was near at hand, a loss that showed in his work as an architect.

Despite his trade, even he had been forced to live in makeshift accommodations after losing his home during the war.

Whether clothing or a house, it was no doubt impossible to design something to match his daughter's natural beauty. Perhaps the ideal life for those blessed with such beauty was to live outdoors in nature, naked as animals? Could it be that new thoughts in architecture always stemmed from this kind of epiphany?

In any event, entering a bath with his daughter for the first time in countless years, watching the movements of her graceful body, as an architect, Mizuhara was deeply moved by a sense of paternal affection, a want to build a house for her in which she could live comfortably. He hadn't considered with whom she might live in that house.

However, he couldn't help but feel a little uncomfortable in her presence. He held himself back in the narrow bathtub, contemplating his lost youth. Perhaps that was why he had used the word *leave?*

Mizuhara left the bathroom first. Returning to their room, he found on the table a sprig of a daphne that Asako must have brought inside.

Earlier, she had seemed unusually cheerful. He too didn't feel quite his usual self.

The guests on the second floor were listening to a recitation of the tragic tale of the lovers Onoe and Itahachi. The song, accompanied by a shamisen, was being sung by a geisha who, judging from her voice, was no longer young.

Asako returned from the bathroom and stood in front of the mirror. It was rare for Mizuhara to see his daughter putting on makeup.

"Father," her image in the mirror called out. "What was it you wanted to talk about?"

"Hmm?"

"You wanted to speak with me about something, no? That's why you asked me to come with you, isn't it? I've been wondering for a while."

Mizuhara remained silent.

"How many houses would you build for us? Two? Three?"

"Why?"

"If it was just Momoko and me, two would be enough. But there's our sister in Kyōto too, isn't there?"

Mizuhara felt his brow furrowing into a frown.

At that moment, a maid entered the room to set out the evening meal.

Asako sat by the hibachi brazier, her gaze downcast as she fiddled with the daphne sprig while the maid arranged the trays and dishes.

The flower had a short tubular corolla, pink in the center, radiating out to a purple-tinged frill. Mizuhara too found his gaze lingering on it.

3

In the morning, the weather was clear, and the waters off Nishikigaura were sparkling.

"Did you hear the Akita barking last night?" Mizuhara asked his daughter.

"No." Asako, having just taken a bath, was sitting in front of the mirror.

"It was so deep, so resonant."

"Oh?"

He began to speak again about Marquis Iga. "Even though he was descended from a feudal lord, the marquis who lived next door had had his privileges taken away even before the war. His debauched lifestyle was an affront to the reputation of the nobility, you see. But he probably has few regrets about enjoying them while he could, seeing as the rest of the nobility was stripped of their wealth and privileges after the war regardless."

When Mizuhara had come to see the marquis's villa so many years before, he had been inclined to appreciate the elegance of the architecture—the buildings being inspired as they were by tearoom aesthetics—and to reflect on his own age; but now that he was staying in the residence next door, he was more inclined to compare his own way of life to that of the former marquis.

Perhaps that was in part because the fates of architects were now at the mercy of the destructive power of the atomic bomb?

The Buddhist words *Throw away this house, throw away that house* passed through his mind.

He left the Camellia House with his daughter. After taking a stroll around the town, the two boarded a bus for Moto-Hakone.

First they crossed Jikkoku Pass, then Lake Ashi came into sight as they approached Hakone Pass. There was still snow on Mount Futagoyama, Mount Komagatake, and Mount Kamiyama.

As they walked along the cedar-lined path toward Hakone Shrine, Mizuhara glanced toward the porter from the mountain inn. "The plums are already in bloom, aren't they?" he asked.

"Not yet. The temperature here is about ten degrees lower than in Atami," the porter answered.

What Mizuhara thought of as *the mountain inn* was the former villa of the main family of the Fujishima conglomerate.

By the entrance of the villa were a waiting room, a garage, and a boathouse.

The room that had been set aside for them was unexpectedly modest. "It really is quite the mountain hut! Was this a dormitory for the staff?" Mizuhara asked as he sat down to warm himself at the *kotatsu* table.

The walls were fitted with plain shōji screens, which hadn't been lined with glass. Beyond was a narrow porch. The entrance was sectioned off from the room by a newly fitted cedar door, which looked to have replaced a fusuma panel.

They made their way to the living room for tea. Guessing that it was a recent addition, Mizuhara was told by the maid that it had been built to replace an old Western-style building that had burned down three years prior.

He nodded to himself in silent understanding. Whatever had remained of the dreams of the Fujishima family must have disappeared with those flames.

They went for a walk through the expansive gardens.

After passing a field of rhododendrons, they arrived at a small tearoom, in front of which spread a field of azaleas.

Next, emerging from a cedar grove, they came to a slightly elevated lawn, upon which towered a tree like a great parasol. Beneath its branches were several benches and a sign with the words *Solitary Cedar*.

The porter guiding them pointed to the shore of the lake. "Do you see those four trees?" he asked. "The lawn over there has been turned into a badminton court."

"Oh, is that Momoko?" Asako began to exclaim before raising a hand to her chest to silence herself.

"Don't shout. And stop looking." There was a tremble to her father's whispered voice.

Momoko was embracing a young man, really no more

than a boy, on one of the benches set out by the four trees. The pair was staring intently at the surface of the lake.

Though he and Asako were then shown to a detached building, and from there to the cottage, Mizuhara was preoccupied by absent thoughts.

There was a sign by the building: *Six-Hundred-Year-Old House from Hida-Takayama*. The English translation read *seven hundred years*.

"An extra hundred years for our foreign guests!" Mizuhara laughed as though trying to lighten the mood.

"They say that Mr. Fujishima used this house when he wanted to serve country food to his guests," the porter told them.

The house looked to be mostly in its original condition, even down to the planks of wood in the stable, stained black perhaps by animal droppings.

The roof, however, had mostly collapsed. Seeing the snow on Mount Kamiyama through the breach in the ceiling, Mizuhara felt a shiver climb up his spine. Asako too looked pale.

They spoke little that evening.

Mizuhara's thoughts passed to Momoko, who it seemed had avoided Yugawara, Atami, and the hot spring resorts in Hakone in favor of a mountain inn during the winter season when there would be few guests.

Being born to a different mother, she resembled Asako only slightly; and so it was unlikely that anyone had realized that they were related.

Momoko certainly couldn't have suspected that her father, who had told her that he was going to Atami just one day earlier, had come now to this inn deep in the heart of Hakone.

4

Momoko hugged the boy from behind.

The boy made no move to embrace her. "Why are you crying?" he asked listlessly.

There was a languid quality to Momoko's voice. "I'm not crying."

"I can feel your tears on my neck."

"Can you? You're too sweet."

The boy began to turn around.

"No. You mustn't look," Momoko whispered, staring at the peony-colored curtains.

The room that the pair had been given was on the opposite side of the inn to the one taken by Mizuhara and Asako. Though it was a Japanese-style room, it had been laid out in a slightly Western style, fitted with a large double bed.

The Color of Flames

I

They could hear the distant sound of a motorboat from their room as they waited for breakfast.

Asako glanced toward her father.

"Someone must be off to collect ration allocations again," he said.

The evening before, they had seen another boat coming back with a load of rations.

Around sundown, the paper of the shōji screen had flickered with the color of flames. When Asako opened the door to look outside, she saw a gardener burning the withered grass. The fire spread in large rings, shimmering like a mirage.

Lake Ashi was still. The line of the far shore was still lit by the lingering dusk, but the mountains that towered above had faded into the twilight. There had been no sunset.

It was then that she saw a boat moving across the water through the gaps between the trees.

"Oh? Who would want to go out in a boat in this cold?" she asked.

The gardener looked toward the lake. "They're coming back with some rations."

"They went for rations on a boat?"

"It's heavier going by land, and it will be a woman from the village rowing."

The boat, passing through the dusk hanging between the trees by the shore, was indeed being rowed by a woman in a plain kimono.

"How nice, being able to go shopping by boat," Asako said, prompted by her uneasiness.

"Shut the door," her father instructed. "It's cold."

As she slid the door closed behind her, the flickering colors of the flames were again projected onto the bottom of the screen.

Asako was restless that morning too as she listened with trepidation to the hum of the motorboat.

"Are you sure they're going for rations? Yesterday it was a rowboat, but this one is a motorboat."

Unconvinced, she opened the screen a fraction and peeked outside. After checking to make sure that Momoko wasn't in the garden, she slid it open fully.

The motorboat was speeding toward Kojiri, in the direction of the cloud-covered reflection of Mount Fuji.

From her vantage point, the boat the night before had looked as though it were weaving between the trees, keeping close to the shore. The motorboat, however, was heading out into the center of the lake, and looked to be practically grazing against the treetops.

"It's Momoko! I was right, it's Momoko!" Asako held tightly to the screen. "She's with that boy, Father! What is she thinking, going out onto the lake in this cold?"

It was a small motorboat, but it left a long trail on the otherwise smooth surface of the water.

Momoko was in the stern, nestling up to the boy.

Even on the mountains of the far shore, thin lines of snow could be seen here and there.

"Father . . ." Asako began as she turned around.

Mizuhara avoided his daughter's beseeching gaze. "Shut the door."

"Yes." She continued, however, to stare after the boat.

"Asako. I asked you to shut the door."

"Yes," she repeated, returning to the *kotatsu* table in a daze.

"What will you do, Father?" she asked after a moment.

Mizuhara remained silent.

"Are you really going to let her do this? Are you? I can still hear it, the motorboat. My heart is beating so! I couldn't sleep at all last night."

"Yes, I know. But even if we tried to catch her here . . ."

"But, Father, where else would we be able to catch her?"

"Maybe it shouldn't be me. Yesterday, no, the day before, when I said I wanted to build a house for you, you said I would have to build one for your sister as well."

"Yes. But I have another sister in Kyōto too, don't I? So I wanted to know how many you would build. Two? Three?"

"Well . . ." Mizuhara began. "Even if I did build one for Momoko, I doubt she would want to live in it."

"Why not? Why would you think only I would want to live in a house you built? Why not Momoko?"

"It's difficult to explain, but maybe because I married your mother."

"What?" Asako shook her head. "That's awful . . . I don't want to hear it. You're being unfair, don't you think?"

"You're probably right." Mizuhara nodded before continuing as though to himself, yet with a clear voice, "I've had two lovers during my life and been married once. I took charge of the child from the first, but not the one from the second. But I suppose you already know about that, don't you?"

Asako was silent for a moment, but couldn't hold down her questions. "Why didn't you take the other child? Was it because of my mother?"

"No. I took the first child because her mother had died. A suicide." Mizuhara spoke as though spitting out poison.

A shadow clouded the beautiful line of Asako's tired eyelids. "Father, even with three daughters by three women, could it be that I'm your only real child?"

"Well . . . ? Thank you for your thoughts, but . . ."

"You sound so sad, Father."

"But whether living together or apart, whether abandoned or entrusted to someone else, one's offspring is after all one's own. The links between parent and child can't be broken."

"Isn't that just like saying a stepmother can never be a real mother? Poor Mother!"

"Children shouldn't pity their parents. To pity others unnecessarily . . . isn't that itself something to be pitied?"

"It's all your fault, Father."

"You're probably right. But I suppose fate isn't the kind of thing that really adds up in the end."

"Are you saying it was *fate* that put Momoko in that motorboat? That this was inevitable?"

"I didn't say that. Do you really think Momoko is serious about that boy?"

"I don't know."

"I did expect her to put more into it. She has her mother's temperament, always going to extremes, always on edge, always finding something to devote herself to, to the exclusion of everything else. But with this boy, it's as if she's given up."

"Given up? She seems to be serious enough. But right now . . . right now, she has two boyfriends, Father. The boy she's with, his name is Takemiya. I don't know what she's thinking, dating two boys at the same time." Asako spoke with reluctance, pulling back to make herself small.

Mizuhara seemed only mildly surprised. "She isn't herself. We have to find out what's hurting her; otherwise, we might not be able to stop her from playing with fire. Do you have any clue what it could be, Asako?"

"What's hurting her? Perhaps that's something she could share only with her real mother?"

"It's more that she's obstinate," Mizuhara deflected. "When someone plays with danger, like chewing on a knife, it's because they're harboring a wound that's eating them from inside. Or maybe it's a way of edging toward suicide."

"*Suicide?* Momoko?" Frightened by those words, Asako found herself shivering.

"I can't hear the motorboat anymore, Father. Could Momoko have a suicide pact with that boy?" Rising on unsteady feet, Asako went to open the shōji screen. "It's not that, is it? Father? I can't see the boat."

Mizuhara felt a sudden chill. "They've just gone out onto the lake."

Asako scanned the water all the way to Kojiri. "But where? I can't see them. I can't make out even a single boat. I'm going down to the shore to look for them." With those words, she slipped into a pair of garden clogs and rushed from the room.

Behind her departing figure rose a faint cloud of ash from the grass burned the previous day.

2

There was only the soft susurrus of snow falling, a faint sound, as though something was gently brushing against the shōji screen.

As the sliding partitions were lined only with paper, the cold and the silence crept into the room all the more.

They had noticed the sound just before noon and, upon opening the screen, had seen that the snow was falling steadily.

The mountains by the far shore had disappeared. The snow obscured almost the entire surface of the lake, painting the trees by the shore a stark white. It had already buried the lawn.

Mizuhara had begun to think that they should leave before they found themselves snowed in, when Asako spoke up. "Let's wait until Momoko goes home first. It would be awkward if we were to run into her, don't you think, Father? That would be sure to upset her."

"It's like we're just hiding here, like we've done something wrong."

"But it's true. It *was* wrong of you to bring only me here."

Waiting for Momoko to depart, warming himself absent-mindedly at the *kotatsu* table, Mizuhara felt a chill climbing up his back. His thoughts turned to his three daughters, so unlike one another but so like their mothers in looks and temperament, even down to the ways in which they lived their lives.

But while each of his daughters resembled their mothers, they had each inherited something from him too. Whether the curve of their ears, the gait of their walk, the shape of their toes, they each had delicate features that, despite their differences, pointed toward their shared father.

The ways in which children born to the same mother tended to resemble their parents, while at the same time differing from them, was indeed curious; but in his case, the fact that his three daughters each resembled their different mothers so remarkably, and at the same time resembled him, seemed to Mizuhara stranger still.

Was it fairer to say that the three women had borne children because of him, or that he had been borne children by the three women? Looking back on his past at an age when it was unlikely that he would father any more offspring, what he felt wasn't bitter remorse but rather that he had been the beneficiary of the grace of heaven and the vitality of woman. More than anything, the overflowing beauty of his three daughters was indisputable evidence that they weren't children of sin.

The mothers of Momoko, his eldest, and Asako, his second, had both passed away.

What else had those two women left to the world, other than their daughters and his memories of their love?

Both of them, and he too, had experienced the pains and sorrows that come with love. But even those feelings now seemed to him to have passed far away, as, of course, they had for the dead women.

His three daughters continued to suffer from the circumstances of their births and their father's past. And yet he was sure of their love for him.

With the passage of the years, he had come to doubt that joy and sorrow, pleasure and pain, were deep truths of the human condition. They had begun to seem to him no more than small, ephemeral waves in the flow of life.

However, his relationship with the mother of his third daughter, a Kyōto woman, differed from those that he had had with the other two.

Before giving birth to his youngest daughter, she had borne a child by another man. And it wasn't impossible that she might have yet more by other men in the future. She was, after all, still alive.

Mizuhara had been the only man in the lives of Momoko's and Asako's mothers.

Even so, he had never felt any resentment between himself, the Kyōto woman, and their daughter. Rather, there was probably a sort of affection between them.

Knowing why Asako had gone to Kyōto, he had invited her to come with him to Atami so that he could have an opportunity to talk to her about her younger sister. But when Asako had raised the subject first, he found himself at a loss for words; and now that they had happened upon Momoko at Hakone, the opportunity had passed.

Nonetheless, it would have been enough for him if Asako had guessed that he had wanted to talk about the Kyōto girl.

Of the mothers of his three daughters, Asako's, Sumiko, was the only one with whom he had felt truly at ease. But now that she had passed away, only the Kyōto woman remained.

The thought of asking Asako her view of it all only made it more difficult for him to speak about his youngest child.

When Asako went to Kyōto in search of her younger sister, had she perhaps hoped to meet the girl's mother too?

As he listened to the sound of the snow falling, Mizuhara felt a sudden nostalgia for the woman, still alive and well in Kyōto.

"Asako. You'll catch a cold if you fall asleep there," he said as he shook his daughter's shoulder.

Asako opened her bloodshot eyes. Resting her arm on the frame of the *kotatsu* table, she turned her face to the floor.

"Is Momoko still . . . ? Maybe we shouldn't let her know we came here? But this must be strange for you too, Father."

"We can't leave with this snow."

"Momoko will have come back to the inn. With all this snow coming down, she won't go out to die, will she?"

"This again?"

"I really thought they were going to die. It's your fault, Father, for talking about suicide."

Recalling the suicide of Momoko's young mother, Mizuhara shook his head.

3

With his back to Momoko, the Takemiya boy took a piece of firewood in either hand and fed them both into the hearth.

"I just remembered the white birch firewood from Karu-izawa," he said as though reciting a line.

Momoko continued to contemplate the snow outside. "Did you live in Karuizawa?"

"Yeah."

"Does it make you sad, remembering it?"

"No. There was nothing sad about it."

"Oh?"

The boy squatted by the hearth, stoking the fire.

"White birch must make poor firewood," Momoko said.

"It's pretty. There's no problem so long as it burns, right?"

"I suppose so. There's no need to cook anything, or make tea with it, after all."

"A White Russian girl kissed me."

"Oh? Someone kissed you before I did?" Momoko faced the boy's turned back. "This is a very serious matter. And just where did she kiss you, Little Miya?"

The boy remained silent.

"And where did you kiss her? In a house in the mountains, in front of a fireplace lit with white birch? What kind of girl was she? A baker's daughter? A wool merchant's daughter? How old was she? Tell me. You have to tell me."

"Tonight."

"Tonight? Do you want to stay here tonight too, Little Miya?"

"We're snowed in. I'd like to visit Atami, though."

"We can't. My father and sister are there."

The boy spun around. Momoko glanced out the window. The boy too turned to look at the snow falling on the surface of the lake.

"The snow is coming down heavily. It would be too dangerous to take a bus through these mountain roads. I wouldn't mind if we fell into a valley, but I'm sure *you* would be saved, and it would only be *me* who died. I couldn't stand that."

"Why do you think you would be the only one to die?"

"Because you don't love me."

"Oh?" Momoko stared at the boy. "Come here."

He sat beside her on the sofa. Momoko put her arms around his shoulders, turning him around so that he lay on her lap. "What did that Russian girl smell like when she kissed your cute mouth, Little Miya?"

"What?" The boy looked dazed.

"They say when a girl is in love, even her breath smells like roses," Momoko said with a gentle smile. "But you were still a child then, weren't you, Little Miya? She must have taken you by surprise, no?" She leaned in close to the boy's face.

"Your nose is cold," he whispered.

"It's because we're so far from the fire, Little Miya."

The boy rested his hands on Momoko's neck, closing his eyes.

"You smell like cigarettes, Little Miya. You'll have to stop smoking."

"Right."

"Make sure you do. I want to smell the scent of first love on your breath."

Momoko put a hand on the nape of his neck, pulling him toward her.

There was a sense of innocence to the short down on his neck, and a youthful freshness to his moist eyebrows and eyelashes.

With her free hand, she ran her fingers through his bangs.

"You're a good liar, Little Miya," she said after a moment. "It's very cute."

"I'm not lying."

"Oh? So the story about the White Russian girl was true? It would have been cuter if it were a lie."

"You're a much better liar than I am."

"Do you think so?"

Momoko wrapped her arm around the boy's back, embracing him.

"You're getting big. You mustn't get any bigger, Little Miya."

"Don't talk nonsense," he murmured, pressing his thumbs into Momoko's neck.

"You're strangling me, Little Miya."

"I know."

"It's okay. Go on, strangle me." Momoko closed her eyes, tilting her head backward as though offering herself to him.

"You're going to abandon me, aren't you?"

"What makes you think that? I'm not going to abandon you."

"Don't abandon me."

"You shouldn't talk like that. It's unmanly."

"Are you just playing with me?"

Momoko took the boy's hands in her own and guided them away from her throat. "There isn't a woman in this world who would play with a man. *That* I know only too well."

Her breathing was ragged, her eyes glistening with tears. There were red marks on her throat where the boy had gripped it.

The boy buried his face in the marks. "But you were just playing with Nishi, weren't you, before you threw him away?"

"Did Nishida say that?"

"He did. He called you a demon, a temptress . . ."

"What a spineless thing to say! I didn't abandon him. It was more like he moved on from me."

"Am I going to *move on* from you too?"

"Only you can decide that, Little Miya. Didn't Nishi run off with a classmate?"

"Only after you were finished with him. They went to an inn in Ikaho that you had taken him to. That's where they were caught."

"I hate the kind of man who would take another girl to a place he had gone with me."

"He probably didn't know anywhere else."

"I suppose you're right. But that's enough talk about Nishi." Momoko put her lips to the boy's head. "What nice hair! It smells much better than your breath. It brings back so many memories."

"Memories? Of what?"

"Of when I was younger . . ."

The boy drew back. "You don't really love anyone, do you?"

Momoko jerked away, but then rested a cheek on his head. "Of course I do."

"Who, then?"

She stared outside at the snow.

"You don't, do you?"

"I do. I love my dad."

"Dad? Meaning . . . ?" The boy abruptly lifted his face.

"My father, of course!"

"What? And I was being serious. You're a good liar."

"It isn't a lie. Of course I love him." Momoko stood up, walking toward the southern side of the room, which was fitted with a glass window overlooking the lake. "But that love is a lot like this snow."

Leaning on the tall glass window, which stretched all the way from floor to ceiling, she watched as the snowflakes fell one after another, a deep ashen haze flowing through her eyes.

Momoko and the boy left on the four-thirty bus that afternoon.

4

Mizuhara and Asako decided to take the six o'clock bus. Two boys from the inn carried their luggage and escorted them under a pair of umbrellas. One stumbled and fell in the snow, breaking the strap of his tall wooden clogs. Mizuhara sent him back inside. The other boy had been barefoot from the beginning.

Evening came early due to the snowfall, and the lights from Moto-Hakone and Hakone seemed to sink into the lakeside.

They waited at Moto-Hakone until seven o'clock, but the six o'clock bus still hadn't arrived. It should have long since left Odawara, but it had yet to make it up the mountain.

"The four-thirty bus is still stuck on the mountain due to an accident. It's already been two and a half hours, what with all this snow," a clerk from the bus company told them.

"Momoko was on that bus!" Asako glanced toward her

father before approaching the clerk. "You said there was an accident?"

"It seems a truck coming up from Odawara slipped and turned over in the snow."

"Did anything happen to the bus?"

"We're not sure. We sent someone to find out, and we've been making inquiries, but there aren't any telephones on the mountain."

Twenty minutes later, they were told, to their relief, that the four-thirty bus was once again on its way.

Later still, they were told that the six o'clock service had been canceled. They were the only ones in the waiting room.

Night had fallen. With the snow as thick as it was, they couldn't travel along the mountain road back to their previous inn, and so went instead to another nearer to the bus stop.

When they asked the maid who came to lay the bedding, they learned that the snow was between a foot and a foot and a half deep.

"This must be what they call a pillow of snow! What a mess we've found ourselves in!" Mizuhara said with a forced smile.

"But the lake is just outside the window. It's a lakeside inn!"

"So it seems."

The wind rose on the water, rattling the shutters and windows. There were two hard mattresses lying in the old narrow room.

The snow was blowing into the hallway.

"It will be hard to sleep in this cold, Father. Shall I lie down next to you?"

"I'm fine."

"I can't sleep tonight either. But do you think Momoko will have made it back all right? I'm worried. To be stuck on the mountain in this snow for three hours . . ." Asako raised her head from her pillow, looking to her father.

Spring in Kyōto

I

Mizuhara decided to take his daughters to Kyōto to see the cherry blossoms.

A client who had settled down in the city after losing his home during the war had requested his services to remodel his new house and design a room for the tea ceremony.

"The Miyako Odori, the spring dance festival, is being held again for the first time in seven years, so he suggested I bring you both along to see the flowers," he told his daughters by way of invitation. "I can take a look at the house while we're there."

Hearing this, Momoko exchanged a quick glance with Asako.

Later, when they were alone, she asked her, "Do you think he might have some other reason for inviting us along?"

Asako nodded. "Maybe he wants to introduce us to our younger sister?"

"Introduce us? Why do you sound so grateful? *I* don't want to meet her."

"But you'll come, won't you?"

"I don't want to."

Asako looked at her sister sadly. "It was only Father and me who went to Atami. Are we supposed to visit Kyōto by ourselves too, leaving you behind like an unwanted stepchild? Poor Father!"

"You're the one who wants to meet her, so *you* should go. *I* don't want to meet her, so there's no need for me to go. Isn't that fair?"

"In that case, it should be you who goes. I'll stay here."

"Dear me! That would really make Father sad."

"But if I don't go, he won't try to introduce you to her."

"What are you saying? It's *me* Father wants her to meet in the first place. After all, you've already accepted her as your sister. You even went looking for her. Don't you think it's because *I* don't want to acknowledge her that he's trying to introduce us?"

Asako shook her head. "You're making this all very difficult!"

"It's a difficult situation." Momoko laughed.

"Is it because of Mother? Because she was a stepmother to you?" Asako spoke lightly, but the smile faded from Momoko's face. Nonetheless, she continued in the same tone of voice, "But since Mother passed away, it seems like your relationship with Father has only worsened. It's almost like you really do believe you're only a stepdaughter. I can't understand it. It's just so heartbreaking."

"Now aren't you the one who's overcomplicating it?" Momoko paused for a moment to regain her composure before addressing her once more. "Asako. I won't let what you're saying bother me too much, because you truly do believe your mother was kind to me, even if I was a stepchild, don't you?"

"Of course."

"All right. Then I'll go with you."

"What a relief!"

"I would hate to seem so stubborn as to grieve a father already mourning the loss of his wife."

"I'm mourning too."

"And so am I."

Asako nodded.

The image of her sister and the Takemiya boy, sitting together in the motorboat as it glided across the surface of Lake Ashi, rose in her mind.

"Maybe Father doesn't mean to introduce us to her. Maybe he really does just want to take us to see the blossoms. It would seem too sad to go alone."

"Maybe," Momoko answered.

The three of them left Tōkyō on the Ginga overnight service at eight thirty in the evening.

As there were so few passengers in the second-class carriages, they took a four-seat compartment for themselves, so that one of them would be able to lie down.

Mizuhara was the first to take the double seat, but he couldn't fall asleep, and so swapped places with Momoko as the train neared Numazu.

Later, after they passed Shizuoka, she said that she too was unable to sleep, and so swapped places with Asako.

"Father, why don't you try to get some rest in a sleeper car?" Momoko suggested. "There must be at least one bed free. Why don't you ask the conductor?"

But for Mizuhara, the opportunity to spend ten hours with his eldest daughter was a rare thing, and one that he didn't want to let go to waste.

Asako was sound asleep.

"She really does look innocent, sleeping so soundly like that," Momoko said.

"I don't think she was able to sleep much when we went to Atami."

Momoko was silent for a moment. She glanced up toward the luggage rack. "Look how used to traveling we've all become, what with such small bags!"

"Indeed. To be able to travel so easily. The world has gone back to normal, hasn't it?"

"But you're used to traveling too, Father. Why can't you sleep?"

"I could, if I felt like it."

"Then you should get some rest!"

"Don't you think you should try as well?"

"But if I go, Asako will say I'm acting like a stepchild again."

"Did she say that?"

"So I told her I wouldn't be offended if she really did believe Mother hadn't treated me any differently than her."

Mizuhara remained silent, his eyes closed.

"We've given her a lot to worry about, haven't we?" Momoko too closed her eyes. "Since Mother passed away, it seems like Asako has taken on all the household responsibilities herself. She's trying so hard to do well by us."

"She is, isn't she?"

"It would be best for her if I left home," Momoko said. But as though those words had come back to pursue her, she hastened to add, "Wouldn't it? I understand that only too well."

"Don't say such things." Mizuhara opened his eyes. "She might hear you."

"She's sound asleep," Momoko answered without looking. "It would be best for her to find a husband soon. I wouldn't want her to repeat my mistakes." She felt a painful warmth beneath her closed eyelids. "But, Father, could you bear to let her go so easily? It would make you too lonely."

"I wouldn't say that."

"It's true. I'm sure of it," Momoko said with a shudder.

She realized with horror that her father was torn between his love for Asako and his love for her. Just as he had been torn between their mothers.

No, she corrected herself. That wasn't true. His relationship with Asako's mother had only begun after that with her own had ended. He hadn't been involved with both women at the same time.

These thoughts, however, weren't enough to extinguish the strange fire that had been kindled in the bottom of her heart.

She was suddenly terrified, as though she could see the flames from beneath her eyelids.

Was it her fate to be possessed by the love of her mother, who had ended her life so many years before?

Had her love for her father and stepmother, and her love for her father and half sister, reached her through her own jealousy and that of her mother?

She pulled herself away from her father and turned to lean against the window. Mizuhara opened his eyes. Momoko couldn't help but feel as though he were staring through her.

He soon dozed off, however.

Asako awoke as the train was passing through Maibara.

Being a good riser, she opened her eyes with a snap and broke into a smile. "Oh no! You were already awake! Were you both watching me sleep without getting any rest yourselves?"

"Young girls do like to sleep in late," Momoko said with a laugh as she looked around.

For the most part, the male passengers seemed to have already refreshed themselves. Momoko too had finished with her makeup.

The water wasn't running in the lavatory, so Asako merely wiped her face with a cream.

She unfastened a button of her blouse and washed the base of her neck. Momoko kept watch, worried that someone might try to steal a furtive glance at her younger sister.

"Turn around for a moment," she urged before fixing her hair for her.

"It's Lake Biwa. Look at the morning mist!" Asako stared out over the water.

"You know it will be a sunny day when the morning is as cloudy as this," Momoko said.

"But there won't be any rainbows with these clouds," Asako sighed.

"Rainbows? Ah, are you thinking about the one you saw at the end of last year, on your way back from Kyōto?"

"Yes. The gentleman on the train said we might see more rainbows appear over Lake Biwa when traveling along the Tōkaidō."

"Oh? The man who won your admiration for looking after his baby so well all by himself?"

"Yes. He said when the fields along the banks of the lake are flowering with rapeseed and milk vetch in spring, seeing a rainbow is happiness itself."

Mizuhara too gazed out the window.

They could see Hikone Castle. Below it stood a grove of flowering cherry trees.

As the train entered Yamashina, the cherry blossoms became more numerous. At last, they had arrived at flowery Kyōto.

The streets of the old capital were lined with red lanterns for the Miyako Odori, and the sides of the streetcars were emblazoned with large notices for the gubernatorial election.

They went to an inn near Sanjō and took to their beds after breakfast to get some rest.

Asako awoke to find that their father had gone out.

She spotted a note left next to her pillow.

I didn't want to wake you; you were both sleeping so well. I've gone to the Daitokuji Temple. I'll be back before evening. Why don't you both go see the Miyako Odori?

To her surprise, her father had left two tickets to the theater.

2

As soon as Mizuhara arrived at the entrance to the Jukōin, a subtemple of the Daitokuji, two black dogs ran out toward him.

The animals were too large to be indoor dogs. They were

almost identical, standing at attention beside one another as he stared down at them. They didn't bark.

Mizuhara found the corners of his lips rising in a faint smile.

"Oh my, Mr. Mizuhara! It's been so long!" exclaimed an elderly woman, the wife of the preceptor. "What a pleasant surprise!"

"Apologies for my long absence," he said. "What interesting dogs. They came out to greet me, and now they seem to be standing like a pair of obedient novices. What breed are they?"

"I wouldn't know," the woman replied absently. "I'm sure they're nothing special."

The woman hadn't changed at all, Mizuhara thought.

She led him to a room inside, knelt to greet him formally, and rose back to her feet. "I'm sorry we can't offer you anything to eat. At least let me bring some flowers." With those words, she brought an arrangement of three large white camellias set in a simple bamboo vase.

Mizuhara was struck by their purity.

"One of them looks like a double flower."

The woman set the vase down on the corner of a small table.

"Have those large camellias in front of the abbot's house bloomed yet? I suppose they've probably already wilted," Mizuhara remarked.

In his mind's eye, the camellias, along with the garden and Mount Hiei behind it, floated up before him.

"I'm sure they still have plenty of flowers. Camellias are long-lived," the woman replied.

Mizuhara glanced idly at a solitary flower in front of him. "What variety is that?"

"I wonder. A fritillary, perhaps?"

"A fritillary? How do you write that?"

"With the characters for *double* and *yam*, I think? Perhaps it's a potato that won't stop growing?" The woman all but brushed the question aside.

Mizuhara realized that he had broken out into another smile.

"A double yam."

It was green in color and looked like a cross between a lily of the valley and a bellflower.

"Are you alone this time, Mr. Mizuhara?" the woman asked.

Only then did he realize that she hadn't heard of his wife's passing.

"Actually . . ." he began uncertainly. "I'm hoping to see Kikue."

"Oh?"

"A woman I came here with once, a long time ago."

"I see." The woman nodded.

"She was carrying a small child back then."

"Yes, yes."

"We've long since parted ways. So I thought it would be best if we could meet at a temple. I'm sorry to bring our worldly affairs into a place like this, though."

"Is she coming here?"

"Probably. I think so."

"I see." The woman didn't seem to mind. "Shall I wait for her to arrive before bringing tea? Let me call the preceptor. He'll know we have a guest. I'm sure he'll be delighted to see you." With that, she left the room.

When the preceptor entered, he dragged one leg behind him as he walked. He looked to be suffering from partial paralysis.

Mizuhara was startled at the sight of his full head of white hair.

His round face, framed by whiskers and a long beard, bore a healthy complexion. His appearance was radiant. His white bushy eyebrows suggested the image of a Taoist hermit more than it did a Buddhist monk.

His flowing beard was braided like a young girl's hair. It hung all the way down to his navel and seemed to glow with golden light.

"Impressive!" Mizuhara gestured as though stroking an imaginary beard.

"I learned it from the Ainu," the preceptor said. "I visited Hokkaidō the year before last, and one of the natives explained that if I tied it like this, it wouldn't get in the way. He was right. It's surprisingly comfortable."

The thick white hair, gathered behind his head in a braid, certainly did call to mind that of an old Ainu man.

"I've become a native myself! A native in the heart of Kyōto!" the preceptor laughed. "And I grew tired of going around bald, so as you can see . . ."

"It looks good on you," Mizuhara replied.

"I used to shave my head by myself, but ever since I took ill, my hand hasn't been as steady as it once was. And the barbershop would want fifty whole yen to shave it all off. Money like that is hard to come by for us simple temple folk in this day and age!" The preceptor let out another laugh.

Beneath those thick white eyebrows, the preceptor's large

dark eyes glimmered with youth. Even that shady hue called to mind an Ainu native; but to Mizuhara, it carried a wave of refreshing purity.

"How old are you, if I might ask?"

"Oh, he's around seventy, I would say," replied the woman.

Mizuhara spoke with the preceptor about their mutual acquaintances in Kyōto, but the old master seemed to have difficulty understanding what he said.

"Are you a little hard of hearing?" Mizuhara asked.

"When was it exactly? I lost my footing on the outdoor passage one day and fell into the garden. I'm sorry to say my ears haven't been what they once were since. People used to say they could hear a bush warbler singing, but I couldn't. But then, one morning, I pinched my nose as I washed my face, and lo! I could hear again."

Mizuhara pricked his ears, hoping to make out the sound of Kikue's soft footsteps approaching. "I can hear one singing now."

The song of a bush warbler reached him through the silence.

"Whenever I come to Kyōto, there are always so many flowers. It's always a relief to come here, to the Daitokuji. There aren't many cherry trees on the grounds, are there?"

"Cherries would spoil the garden," the preceptor said.

"The petals would scatter all over the place, and the leaves would make a downright mess," the woman added.

"Cherry blossoms are too gaudy for a temple," the preceptor continued. "Think of the trouble it would cause if the monks got drunk on all those lively colors!"

The preceptor explained that there was only a single

cherry tree at the Daitokuji, the Konoe Cherry, planted by a former head of that noble house long ago.

As he listened, Mizuhara tried to imagine Kikue walking along the stone path beneath the pine trees.

How, he wondered, might she have changed since he had last seen her?

Black Camellias

I

Kyōto women are renowned for their graceful feet and soft lips. Their skin is said to be beautiful, which Mizuhara certainly thought was true of Kikue's.

Sitting across from the old preceptor, he found himself remembering Kikue's soft lips.

Smooth and tender, those lips seemed to adhere to his. One touch had been enough to make him feel as though he were caressing her entire body.

But the teeth that had once bitten those lips had long since fallen out, replaced now by dentures.

Was it possible that her lips had lost their suppleness too?

"How are your teeth?" Mizuhara asked the preceptor all of a sudden.

"My teeth? Natives have strong teeth," the old master declared, flashing Mizuhara a full set from amid his thick beard. "As robust as a native's, as you can see! No, since the end of the war, it's the buildings of the Daitokuji here that have fallen into disrepair. As decrepit as an old man's teeth. In a decade's time, no doubt they won't even be a shadow of what they once were."

The woman also complained that children lately were all but destroying the temple grounds. The damage caused when they played baseball was apparently the most serious by far.

"There's a bird figure in the main gate, a national treasure from the Momoyama period, but one of those baseballs hit it so hard the wings snapped clean off. And now the head has gone missing too."

"That's terrible," Mizuhara said.

"These *après-guerre* children are like raging bulls, always breaking this and that. They don't listen to anyone. It's madness to grant anyone this much freedom!"

It seemed somewhat discordant to hear the preceptor's wife, dressed in a navy-colored cotton apron like a firewood peddler from Ōhara, use a word like *après-guerre*.

A small sports field had been constructed to the south to prevent the local children from playing baseball within the temple grounds, but the result had been that the wall of the nearby subtemple had suffered damage so horrific that the temple couldn't afford the repairs. The balls, she said, often fell into the temple gardens; and each time the children scrambled up the walls to retrieve them, they would break the tiles in the process.

In the past, the preceptor explained, the precinct in front of the Daitokuji had been home to those who depended on the temple in one form or another for their livelihoods.

Lately, however, displaced families had begun to move in, and their children didn't have the same level of knowledge or respect for the ancient religious complex.

"Even automobiles have started pouring into the grounds. The monks find it convenient to drive right up to the door. There used to be a crosspiece below the gate to stop cars passing through, but they've gone and removed it."

As the preceptor recounted the decay for which the temple seemed destined, he nonetheless retained the serene aspect of a mountain in spring.

Mizuhara felt an urge to speak to him of Kikue. "The way you talk about the temple, you almost sound like someone fondly remembering an old lover," he almost said, but resisted the temptation.

Kikue's hair wasn't red, exactly, but her eyebrows seemed lighter than usual in color, as though lacking pigmentation. Perhaps that explained her pale complexion?

Then again, it could also be said that the faint tint of her eyebrows, her beautiful legs, her soft lips had all made it easier for Mizuhara to leave her.

In fact, those physical qualities had made her seem like a woman with a light, shallow personality, easy to put behind him.

Afterward, Mizuhara would occasionally take notice of other Kyōto women whose features resembled Kikue's. But she had a distinctive way of speaking; while her lips and gums certainly didn't protrude, she tended to reveal them when she spoke, a mannerism that accentuated the smoothness of her lips.

Those lips were a pale, luminous red. Mizuhara had often wondered whether Kikue and other Kyōto women wore a different type of lipstick from those in Tōkyō, but it seemed to be her lips themselves that were different. Both her gums and tongue were an unblemished peach-like color.

Whenever he saw another woman with a mouth like that, it was Kikue who came to mind; and while such a sight never failed to rekindle his sense of regret, it would fill him also with an overwhelming urge to reach out to her.

He wanted to tell the preceptor about her, but the chance had already passed him by. He turned his gaze to the shadows of the trees projected across the garden moss.

At that moment, the old master's wife rose to her feet. "She's here."

Mizuhara's heart clenched with emotion. Strangely, his sense of guilt was directed not at Kikue but at his late wife, Sumiko. He felt almost as though she were still alive, as though he had made the journey here to meet a lover in secret, behind her back. It was an unexpected, startling feeling.

Kikue greeted the preceptor first, before turning to Mizuhara. "Did I make you wait? Welcome back," she said, still averting her eyes.

"Did you see the dogs? They must have given you a fright, no?" Mizuhara asked.

"It was a cat this time," the preceptor's wife said offhandedly. "But cats aren't particularly sociable. It just snuck across the floor and slipped out."

Kikue's lips curled in a smile. "The dogs were watching from a distance."

"I see."

"Alas, this place has become an abode for cats and dogs," the preceptor said in jest. "But it's better than foxes and raccoon dogs!"

The old master stared blankly at Kikue, but he didn't seem to remember her.

His wife, catching sight of Kikue's unease, spoke up. "I was waiting for you to arrive before serving tea." She turned to Mizuhara. "Shall I show you to the tearoom?"

"Please." Mizuhara rose to his feet.

The woman led them to a room three tatami mats in size, the very room where the tea master Rikyū was said to have committed seppuku on the orders of the warlord Toyotomi Hideyoshi.

"Would you prepare the tea?" the woman asked Kikue. "It's rather complicated, so I'll leave everything you need laid out on a tray."

"And the preceptor?" Mizuhara asked.

"He can't move very well, so don't mind him. I'll leave everything here." With that, the woman left.

Mizuhara listened to Kikue stirring the tea whisk in the dim light.

"I've missed you," came a hushed voice. "All your telegram said was to come to the Jukōin. If you had let me know what time your train was coming, I would have gone to meet you at the station. Were you with someone?"

"Yes. I brought my daughters with me."

"Oh!" Kikue looked up at him. "Are you here to see the cherry blossoms?"

"We arrived this morning. I slipped out while they were both asleep."

"Don't say that. How awful." She turned the tea bowl slightly on her palm. Her hands were trembling.

Mizuhara picked up one of the candied soybeans that had come with the tea.

Kikue approached him on her knees. "If this wasn't Rikyū's own tearoom, I would break down in tears."

Mizuhara glanced around the room. He could sense something approaching.

"I'm scared, being alone with you here. I could almost die." Kikue sighed. "Do you remember when we came here on the commemoration of Rikyū's death?"

"Yes. When was it again?"

"Years ago, on the twenty-eighth of March. You don't remember, do you? You're so unreliable."

2

"Is that a crape myrtle?" Kikue asked, looking up at the tree on the right-hand side of the garden.

"It's a *sala* tree," the preceptor's wife answered in a loud voice. "The leaves are different from those of a crape myrtle. And the branches are more impressive too."

"So that's a *sala* tree?"

"They say it withered when the Buddha passed away. That's where it gets its white leaves. You can see it in pictures of Nirvana."

"How auspicious."

"The flowers are large and pure white in color. Seeing them fall evokes the opening to *The Tale of the Heike*: *The sound of the Gion Shōja bells echoes the impermanence of all things; the color of the* sala *flowers reveals the truth that the prosperous must decline.* They bloom, and then, in the evening, they fall."

"You mean they bloom in the morning, and fall the same evening?" Mizuhara asked.

"Yes." The woman sat down on the veranda outside the abbot's quarters.

She must have come to see why the two of them hadn't returned from the tearoom.

She had found them sitting on the veranda and opened the shōji screens so that they could admire the painted fusuma panels, before taking a seat at a distance.

Mizuhara sat at the edge of the garden. He had already seen the ornate panels and the stonework in the garden, so gave them only a cursory glance.

Kikue sat behind him.

"There's another *sala* tree near the wall," the woman said. "It's descended from this one here, but it was born in Japan, not India. I wonder what kind of flowers it will have."

"Hasn't it bloomed yet?" Mizuhara asked, glancing toward the young tree.

The branches weren't twisted, but straight, like those of a poplar.

"Not yet," the woman responded before turning discreetly to Kikue. "Don't dwell too much on worry. Life brings tears at times, joy at others."

Kikue, taken by surprise, turned her head.

"However you look at it, the world is a harsh place. You won't get anywhere if you're always straining yourself. Please, take it easy."

"You're right. Thank you."

"It's nothing. Nothing at all. We all torment ourselves over matters of little import."

"How true! But it's not easy for someone like me to find

enlightenment. Though I would like to drop by more often to listen to the old master's teachings."

"The preceptor only looks enlightened because he has nothing else to do. He's reached an age where he's free from work and desire. You'll know what that feels like yourself if you live long enough."

"It wouldn't bode well if old folks still had violent passions!"

"Yes, yes. Money isn't the only form of greed. Do you sometimes wonder why you were born a woman?"

"Well . . ."

"I thought as much," the old master's wife said abruptly before walking away.

Kikue stared at the corner of the veranda where the woman had been sitting until just a moment earlier. "She seemed so nice at first, but then it was like she was reproaching me. I felt so embarrassed. What did you tell her about me?"

"Nothing. Only that I was waiting for you."

"I see. I wonder if she saw through me. I'm so haggard, and look how I'm dressed. But it can't be helped. Who did you tell her you were meeting?"

Mizuhara found himself reluctant to confess that he had described her as a woman with whom he had parted ways.

"It was almost like she thought I was going to seduce you, like she was trying to warn me off. How ridiculous." Kikue glanced toward him, forcing a smile.

Mizuhara didn't feel tempted in the least.

She was simply a woman whom he had once known; no more, no less. The figure sitting before him had all but erased his mental image of the Kikue from his past.

To say that he was disillusioned would be an understatement.

Yet the current Kikue wasn't entirely unlike her past self. Those clear brown eyes that used to shine when he embraced her had dulled slightly. Her mouth had changed faintly, its contours now somewhat looser. Perhaps her nipples, the same peach color as her lips, had likewise wizened. Yet she was still younger than her years. She wasn't nearly as haggard as she claimed.

Mizuhara wondered whether the years had left them estranged.

It felt as though a wall of time now stood between the two of them, as though he were encountering here not Kikue but those very years that they had spent apart.

Had time brought everything to a resolution? Would time wear it all away?

They had severed their bonds cleanly, so he shouldn't have felt any sense of disquiet at meeting her again like this. Nonetheless, he was struck by a feeling of cheerlessness, along with a sense of guilt.

He tried to warm his heart with fond memories of Kikue as she had been, of the intimacy they had once shared.

But unexpectedly, it was the image of his departed wife that rose before him, more alive than ever.

He wondered whether the loss of the much-closer intimacy that he had shared with Sumiko had caused him to grow apart from Kikue too.

He couldn't be sure what she was thinking right now. Were her words truly spoken from the heart?

He felt an impatient desire to draw yet closer to her.

"My wife died last year," he said all of a sudden.

"Oh my!" Kikue stared across at him in surprise, her eyes awash in sorrow. "I see . . . I wasn't exactly sure why, but I

thought you looked downhearted. I'm sorry for your loss."
Her troubled face looked like it was about to cry. "I was worried something was wrong. How terrible."

"Of the mothers of my three daughters, only you still live."

"Only the dregs, you mean? That has an awful ring to it. You mustn't say such things."

"When I'm gone, you'll be the only woman left who remembers me."

"Don't scare me like that! What's gotten into you? You must be terribly lonely."

"I suppose I am."

Kikue peered across at him.

"I'm not saying this because I want you to think better of me once I'm gone, but I should have taken better care of you. I'm sorry."

"What are you saying? You should save those sentiments for your wife. You treated me very well. Not a day has gone past when you haven't been on my mind."

Mizuhara had tried to apologize to Kikue, but it was as she said; he felt as though those words had been directed to his late wife.

"Why did you want to see me again, now that your wife has passed on? You must tell me, or I won't be able to rest. And what would your daughters think if they knew about all this?"

Mizuhara was at a loss for an answer.

"How terrible!" Kikue shook her head.

After a drawn-out silence, the two of them stood up.

"Perhaps we could take a look at Rikyū's grave," Mizuhara suggested when they reached the entrance.

"Ah. I'll let you inside," said the preceptor's wife, bringing a key to open a wooden gate in the garden.

Standing in front of the gravestone, Kikue asked, "Have you built a resting place for your wife?"

"No, not yet."

"I see. Did she ever visit Rikyū's grave? I'll pray to her here." So saying, she placed her hands together and whispered, "Please forgive me."

Kikue was a mystery to Mizuhara. He couldn't discern where custom ended and true feeling began.

She may have been his woman once before, but now she was no doubt receiving the favor of another man.

3

Leaving the Jukōin, Mizuhara and Kikue made their way along a path leading to a small rise on the western edge of the temple complex. Farther along was the Kohōan, a hermitage constructed by the artist Kobori Enshū.

Mizuhara had walked the path leading westward from the Kohōan up to the Kōetsuji Temple in Takagamine once before.

He paused for a moment to contemplate the quiet shadows of the pines and bamboos now projected across the straight path.

A row of subtemples lined the northern side of the road.

"The old master looked rather strange, wouldn't you say?" Kikue remarked.

"He considers himself a native. He said he was imitating an Ainu."

"Is that so? Now that's unusual."

"His commemorative portrait will certainly be an interesting sight."

"His what?"

"Zen monks often have paintings commissioned, portraits to pass on to their disciples. It's an old tradition."

"Oh? I'll have to remember that. I've never seen someone with a beard plaited into three braids."

"He's an odd character, isn't he?"

"Neglecting his appearance like that, letting his hair grow out so long . . . But I suppose it doesn't look all bad. It does frame his face rather well."

"He was rather handsome as a young monk. There was even talk that he might become the chief abbot of the Daitokuji, but instead he was swept away by the waves of this floating world."

"I suppose those who taste life's pleasures and pains in their youth do tend to mellow with age and find enlightenment. Don't they say that earthly desires are the purest path to illumination?"

Mizuhara approached the gate leading into the Sōken'in, the mortuary subtemple built to commemorate the great warlord Oda Nobunaga.

"The camellias must be in bloom," he said before stepping inside.

A large camellia tree, said to have been treasured by Nobunaga's successor Toyotomi Hideyoshi, was flowering on the other side of a barley field.

The garden must have been turned into a field during the war. The great camellia was set off brilliantly by the swaying ears of unripened barley.

"It's been fifteen years since we last came here. I was carrying Wakako in my arms," Kikue said. "There was no one else in the garden then either. Wakako was so happy to see all the flowers. But I'm sure you've forgotten."

"No, I remember." For a moment, Mizuhara was caught by the impression that the great camellia before them was blooming in a far-off world.

"If only we could unwind the clock, go back to that moment," Kikue remarked. "How wonderful to be as young as I was back then!"

"So it would only be me who aged? That would be a little awkward."

"I wouldn't mind. Age doesn't mean all too much to men. It would be enough just for me to be young again."

"That's a rather selfish thing to say."

"It's you men who are selfish. Examine your own conscience. Of course, we women tend to become more complicated as we get older, but even so . . ."

"And you . . ." Mizuhara began, his voice becoming more formal in tone. "How have you been, since we last came here?"

"Thank you for your concern. Oh, I got by, somehow," Kikue replied evasively. "It's the human condition that we endure hardship. There's no such thing as a perfect moment in time."

Mizuhara no longer had any right to meddle in Kikue's life. Nonetheless, he couldn't help but suspect that, being in the courtesan trade, she must have had a difficult time supporting herself and her two daughters during and after the war.

"My wife was concerned about Wakako right up until she passed," he said.

"Was she? How kind of her. But you'll make me feel like I've done her wrong. I'll have to pay my respects on the anniversary of her death."

To Mizuhara, Kikue's words seemed rather superficial.

"I've given Wakako a decent upbringing," she said as though speaking about someone else's child. "Although her elder sister has had to endure a lot for her sake."

"How is she, by the way? Your eldest?"

"Yūko? She's already made her debut."

Her debut as a geisha, no doubt.

Mizuhara stepped away from the large camellia, leaving through the gate.

"Yūko has never had an easy life, not since she was a child. Maybe that's why she's always been rather cold. She doesn't have much affection for her sister," Kikue confided as they walked. "Wakako, though . . . she has a gentle spirit."

"You should have brought her with you."

"I wanted to, but I didn't know whether you wanted to see her."

"I suppose it would be somewhat awkward to proudly introduce myself as her father."

"What are you saying? Do you think she's forgotten how you pampered her as a child? When I told her I was going to see you, she followed me all the way out to the street with tears in her eyes."

"I see."

"Yūko gave birth to a baby girl last year. The father is a

strange one. He's still so young, and single too, yet he took the baby back to Tōkyō with him and plans to raise her by himself. Every now and then, he brings her back to Kyōto to see her mother. It's a sight, I say, seeing him traveling by train with the child in his arms. He even offered to marry my Yūko. He's too good for her. I tell her she's been blessed, that her stubbornness will bring misfortune down on her head, but she won't listen. It's fine, I tell her, I won't make Wakako work in her place. I'll take care of Wakako, I tell her, because I love her father. But no matter what I say, Yūko is just too obstinate. Even when the father brings the child with him, she hesitates even to pick the poor thing up. Wakako is a much better babysitter. I feel so sorry for the child that I can't stand it sometimes. I even tried to remind the father that the girl is the daughter of a geisha, that there's no way of telling whether she's even truly his, that he could very well abandon her if he so pleased. Besides, *I* raised two daughters all by myself, with no father to help me. But he wouldn't listen either. I even told Wakako to take the child, to run off with her, that if she did that, he would have to give up and accept reality. But she wouldn't."

Mizuhara winced. Kikue probably didn't mean to compare him with that commendable father, but her comments stung all the same.

He wondered whether this was the same man whom Asako had met during her train journey back from Kyōto around the New Year.

It was clear from this story that Kikue hadn't had any other children after Wakako and that she truly cared for their daughter.

"It just so happens he brought the child again the day

before yesterday. They're off to see the Miyako Odori later today."

"Oh? My daughters should be going too."

"Is that so? What a coincidence," Kikue seemed taken aback. "They might even bump into each other. What to do? Wakako will be with him, looking after the baby. She might meet your daughters."

"She could at that."

"Is that all you have to say? Well, I'm not happy. Not at all. Say they won't recognize each other all you want, passing your own siblings by unawares would simply be too cruel. I'm sorry, but I hope Wakako doesn't see them. I would much prefer she meet only with you."

"That's what I've been meaning to ask . . ." Mizuhara began. "I brought my other daughters with me hoping to introduce them to Wakako."

"Is that so?" Kikue was strangely calm. "Because your wife passed away?"

Mizuhara felt a cold stab. "Not exactly. Last year, Asako came to Kyōto to look for her, without telling me or her elder sister."

"Did she now? I had no idea," Kikue startled, before adding coolly, "They do say that ignorance is to know Buddha. Although it would have been better if she hadn't. I don't want anyone coming after my daughter."

"She didn't come to probe. She did it out of an abundance of love, so much so that she didn't even tell me. And she must also be grieving her mother."

Kikue nodded. "I'm sorry. I'm a cynical woman. It's all so unexpected. I'm not quite ready to accept it just yet."

"I would like you to consider it, though."

"Yes, well. Wakako is born of her mother and father," Kikue said, coming out with a startling Buddhist expression. "But are you saying you want to take her away from me?"

"Not as such . . ."

"I see. Wakako has her own life, her own destiny. But I can assure you she hasn't forgotten her father."

"Oh? I'm blessed. I have three daughters born of different mothers, each of whom loves me in their own way."

"Don't let it get to your head. They're women; they'll get by."

The two laughed, exchanging glances. Only then did they realize that they had been standing in the same place for some time.

The shadows cast by the bamboos nearby reached across their feet.

They passed through the gate leading into the Ryūshōji subtemple. Maples stretched out on either side of the path built from rectangular paving stones, their tender branches reaching out. The green glow was so bright that it was all but projected onto the ground.

Mizuhara had met the old monk of the Ryūshōji in Shanghai once during the war.

He was considerably younger than the preceptor of the Jukōin, and much more proper in appearance too. On this fresh encounter, he recounted to his guests his memories of China and explained how Zen had become a fashionable subject of inquiry in America.

Having been invited to try a homemade dish of bamboo shoots from the nearby grove, Mizuhara began to make his way to the tearoom.

"Ah, a black camellia," he said, approaching a flower hanging from the wall.

"It's a shame there are no good buds," the old monk said behind them. "I found a branch this morning with a perfect bud, but when I came back to pick it, it was gone. I've circled the tree more times than I can count, but I can't find it anywhere. It was in the corner of the garden, so I wouldn't expect a flower thief to have taken it. Such a pity."

The branches in the bamboo vase also had a few buds. Yet no doubt the old monk would have preferred to show Mizuhara that perfect black camellia. The buds were a darker shade of black than the flowers, though their color would fade in spring, the old monk explained. They were best at their darkest.

They were small, elegant flowers, their thick petals almost resembling the scales of a pinecone.

After leaving the Ryūshōji, they made their way to the tearoom at the Kōtōin subtemple, said to have been relocated from Rikyū's private residence.

"Is that an aster among the white globeflowers?" Mizuhara asked, contemplating the flowers in the tokonoma alcove.

"Indeed it is," the old monk answered.

The aster was similar in shape to a wild chrysanthemum.

"I suppose you don't have raccoon dogs in Tōkyō?" the old monk remarked. "We have a den of them under the floorboards here."

"Oh? How many?"

"Three, I should say. They often come out to play in the garden."

Mizuhara stepped outside, spotting a wooden door at the

back of the garden with a small hole cut into the bottom to allow the raccoon dogs to venture into the grove.

In the garden, he paid his respects at the grave of the feudal lord Hosokawa Yūsai.

"A stone lantern for a tomb. Rikyū's grave was nice too. I envy them," he said.

He walked around the stone lantern until he laid eyes on a chipped piece.

"I'd like to take a petal home with me," Kikue said over his shoulder.

"From the camellia?" Mizuhara was carrying the flowering branch from the Ryūshōji.

"I'd like to show it to Wakako."

"Ah!" he exclaimed, handing it to her.

"One petal is all I need," Kikue protested, plucking just that from one of the corollas.

Mizuhara had asked the old monk whether he could take the branch, saying that he wanted to show it to his daughters.

Flower Braziers

I

Asako slipped quietly out of the room while her sister slept.

In the corridor, she happened across a maid, who asked her whether she wanted to wash her *honorable face*.

The maid led her to a washroom, switched on the lights, ran some water, and pulled shut the curtain.

The washroom was divided into compartments for three people, and each had mirrors on three sides.

While washing her *honorable face*, Asako smiled to herself as she remembered the *honorable eddoes* and *honorable beans* that had been part of her breakfast. The Kyōto-style eddoes and beans had indeed been wonderfully tender, but the bamboo shoots and yuba tofu skin had been more tender still, and for whatever reason, they weren't referred to as *honorable bamboo shoots* or *honorable yuba*.

With Momoko still asleep, Asako thought to call on the

friend with whom she had stayed when she had last come to Kyōto, but without knowing the real reason why her father had brought them here, and without knowing her sister's true feelings either, the thought of causing any unintended difficulties filled her with a sense of disquiet.

She went back to their room and started looking at the guidebook describing the Miyako Odori, when Momoko asked, "Where's Father?"

Asako glanced over her shoulder. "Are you getting up?"

"Not yet. I was the only one who couldn't get any sleep on the train. Even Father was able to doze off."

Asako passed her sister the note their father had left.

"Oh? The Daitokuji?" Momoko asked dismissively.

"How awful, disappearing the minute we arrived!"

"It's fine. It means we're free to do as we like."

Asako looked toward her sister.

"You should go and see the Miyako Odori. I'll stay here and sleep a while longer."

"But it's already twelve thirty!"

Momoko counted the hours with her fingers. Despite mumbling that she had slept but four, she decided to get out of bed.

Asako showed her the guidebook for the Miyako Odori, suggesting that she come. Though reluctant, Momoko agreed.

The Miyako Odori had been held annually since 1872, but was suspended in 1943 due to the war. This spring was the first time that it had been held in seven years, Asako told her.

"It says that those red lanterns hanging in rows from the eaves of the houses are to indicate that the Miyako Odori is being held, and to announce that the cherry trees are in bloom."

"Oh? I came to Kyōto on a school trip back when I was a girl and asked the *maiko* to give me their autographs," Momoko said. "It was such a peaceful time."

Perhaps Asako had yet to learn that her youngest sister too had been born in such an entertainment district?

It seemed that she was unaware of her younger sister's background. Her late mother had hidden it well, Momoko thought. Even she knew only a little.

Momoko had her doubts about whether her father would have broken off his relationship with the Kyōto woman if the war hadn't broken out. The conflict must have created an inevitable barrier between the two.

But what could he be thinking now? What ulterior motive could he have for sending them alone to see the Miyako Odori in the very district where their younger sister had been born? Momoko couldn't help but feel humiliated.

She knelt at the dressing table and began to flick through the guidebook. Asako sat down beside her, helping to tidy up her loose hairs.

The first elementary school in Japan was opened in 1869 in the Ishidanshita district of Gion. In the confused period following the Meiji Restoration, geisha and *maiko* had been designated *women workers,* and the offices from which they worked had been termed *women worker patronage companies.*

The first international exhibition in Japan was held in Kyōto from the autumn of 1871 through to the spring of 1872. The dances held as part of that exhibition were the beginning of the Miyako Odori.

"During the war, geisha were forced to become *women workers* all over again, being mobilized to take part in labor activities. Only this time, they were called *workwomen,*"

Momoko explained secondhand. Then, under her breath, she continued, "But now the war is over, even in this new world, *maiko* still have to wear those dangling obi sashes."

"It's the symbol of a *maiko*," Asako said. "But I read in the morning newspaper that some of the girls serving tea at the Miyako Odori aren't old enough. It's against the labor laws."

"Those dangling obis are just like a sumō wrestler's top-knot. It's a strange thing, when you stop to think about it, isn't it?"

"Yes, it is quite strange. But it would be even stranger if sumō wrestlers were without their topknots. And there's something odd about the shaved heads and robes of monks too."

"And there are other things in our lives, other things in our hearts, just like those topknots and dangling obis. All sorts of things . . ." Momoko's voice trailed off as she rose to her feet, deftly knotting her own obi.

"But there isn't much difference between a *maiko*'s dangling obi and your own, is there?" Asako asked.

"Exactly. It's mimicry when you follow the latest fads, but it's also mimicry to let yourself be shackled by tradition or convention. There's no way out of it. Although I suppose they do say that imitation detracts from beauty."

Asako picked up the hairs that her sister had left balled up on a corner of the dressing table and threw them into the wastebasket.

"What are you doing? I can do it myself!" Momoko, frowning, stared down at her younger sister.

2

Both the Shinkyōgoku and the Kawaramachi districts were bustling with crowds, so after crossing the Great Bridge at Sanjō, the two sisters took a detour by Nawate Street as they made their way to Shijō.

The bridge had been newly rebuilt. The handrailing was made from wood and decorated with ornamental bronze caps. The bronze statue of Takayama Hikokurō had been removed.

As she looked out toward Kitayama at the misty upper reaches of the river, over the verdure of the willows on the far shore, and to the nearby slopes of Higashiyama, alive with fresh leaves and flowers, Momoko felt the spring of Kyōto.

The theater in which the Miyako Odori was normally held, the Kaburenjō, was being used by a film company as a cinema, and so the dances were to be held this year at the Minamiza.

Even the tearoom didn't have the same atmosphere as when the Miyako Odori had been held in the Kaburenjō, taking place as it was in a dreary Western-style room complete with tables and chairs. Several newly graduated geisha were serving the tea.

The customers were waiting on long narrow benches lined up in a row.

Asako began to sit down on a round seat when she let out a small cry.

The eyes of the man across from her lit up in recognition. "The young lady from the train!" he said with a bow of the head.

Sitting but three seats away was Ōtani, the baby she had seen him with on the train being held in the arms of a young woman to his right.

Ōtani sipped his tea, then rose suddenly to his feet and approached Asako.

"You recognized me right away! And the baby, did she remember me too?"

The man smiled noncommittally.

Asako looked away from Ōtani, turning toward the baby. "And how is she?"

"Very well, thank you." Then, he called out, "Wakako! Wakako!"

The woman holding the baby bowed her head seemingly by reflex. She had begun to walk right past them, only turning back when Ōtani called out to her.

"This is the young lady who was so nice to Chiiko on the train back to Tōkyō at the end of the year."

Wakako, slightly embarrassed, bowed silently.

"My, how she's grown!" Asako exclaimed.

Wakako bent down to show her the child; but at that moment, a geisha brought her a cup of tea.

"Sorry to bother you. We might see you later," Ōtani said before leaving the room.

When the two sisters stood to leave, they were each given a plate by one of the geisha to keep as mementos.

Asako wrapped the two plates, both decorated with a picture of a *dango* dumpling, in a handkerchief.

3

As they left the tearoom, Momoko asked her sister who the girl holding the baby was to Ōtani.

"I don't know. At first, I thought she was the baby's mother and that Mr. Ōtani was looking after the baby because she's still so young. But it looks like I was mistaken."

"My goodness! One look should be enough to tell you she's still a girl. Having a child at that age would be too cruel! Yet I can't help but feel like I've seen her somewhere before."

"Oh? Where?"

"In a movie. She looks a little like the *maiko* from *Thirteen Nights of Love*, don't you think?"

"The one played by Orihara Keiko?" Asako asked. "Do you think so? I don't think she looked quite as sad or as cold."

"That's because she's so young. Probably around sixteen or seventeen? And of course, she's pretty and plump."

"Maybe there *is* a certain similarity . . ."

"And I didn't expect Mr. Ōtani to be like that. From the way you described him, I pictured him as more effeminate. But he's very manly."

"What?"

"And he was taking care of the baby so well."

Other members of the audience were waiting in a lounge.

Being a relatively short show, the Miyako Odori was held four or five times each day. The audience had to wait for the previous session to end before they could enter the theater.

The walls of the waiting room were decorated with paintings of birds and flowers, and with poems written on strips of colored paper, all works of the geisha. They were rather conventional, but not without taste.

While Momoko and Asako were inspecting the artworks, Ōtani rose from the far sofa and approached them once more.

"Please. Won't you sit?" he beckoned.

"Oh, we're fine," Asako replied.

Wakako, still holding the baby in her arms, rose from the sofa and offered them her place.

Ōtani repeated the invitation, and so Asako allowed herself to follow them. "We're all right," she insisted. "You're with a baby, so please, you should sit."

Wakako glanced toward Ōtani in apparent consternation.

He pressed the girl's shoulder slightly, urging her to take the seat.

"But what a coincidence! To think we would see each other again, at the Miyako Odori of all places! Are you in Kyōto to see the show?" There was a touch of suspicion in his voice.

Asako smiled. "Would that be so strange?"

"More unexpected than strange."

"But you're bringing the baby to watch it too?"

"No. Actually, I was hoping to show the young lady here." Ōtani laughed, glancing toward Wakako.

Wakako blushed, her cheeks dimpling. For a moment, she looked as though she wanted to say something, but she held her tongue.

"But you're right. The Miyako Odori isn't the kind of thing you would show a baby," the man continued. "Ah yes! Back then, you scolded me for pointing out a rainbow to her, right?"

"No! I said she would be so happy to be shown a rainbow by her father at such a young age."

Hearing Ōtani's nostalgic tone, Asako felt able to speak freely, but they were, after all, no more than strangers who had once traveled together by train.

Realizing that she had yet to introduce her, Asako motioned toward Momoko. "We were on the train this morning, going past Lake Biwa. I told my sister about the rainbow we saw last year."

"Ah, I thought you must be siblings."

Ōtani turned to Momoko, who approached with a bow of her head.

"This is Mr. Ōtani," Asako said by way of introduction.

"Your sister was very kind to Chiiko back on the train," he said to Momoko.

"Oh? She's kind to everyone. She can be quite pushy about it. Really, she can be such a nuisance."

Ōtani startled. He stared for a long, hard moment at Momoko's face, seemingly taken by surprise.

Only as Momoko stared back reservedly did he look away.

He felt as though her searing gaze had bored deep into him. The image of her white forehead remained vivid in his mind.

Asako leaned toward the child. "She must have turned one already. You said she was nine months old back then."

Wakako began to shift the baby from her lap toward Asako.

"No, it's okay. I wouldn't want to wake her," Asako said, toying with one of the baby's earlobes with the tip of her finger.

She felt a wave of tenderness upon catching the characteristic scent of babies, mixed with the fragrance wafting from Wakako's hair.

"Such cute ears!"

"She gets them from her mother," Wakako said.

The two of them exchanged glances. Their faces were so close that Asako could feel the warmth of the other girl's breath.

Wakako was wearing a light touch of makeup, making the complexion of her ears stand out all the more against her face powder.

Her eyes were a clear light brown, with a childlike warmth.

Even the color of the outer edge of her irises was lighter than usual. They seemed to draw Asako inward.

Ōtani spoke up over their heads. "This young lady is the younger sister of Chiiko's mother. Well, I suppose you might say she's the kinder of the two, to Chiiko at least."

Momoko's ears pricked up. "Are you saying older sisters aren't kind?"

"Maybe," he replied.

Wakako suddenly glanced up toward Momoko, who seemed not to notice.

"But how do you know my name?" Ōtani asked. "Did I hand you a business card?"

"No." Asako felt her cheeks blushing slightly. "I saw the nameplate on your trunk."

"Oh? You have a sharp eye!" He looked surprised. "Well, allow me to introduce myself properly." So saying, he held out a business card.

Momoko, still standing, looked to her younger sister as though wanting to ask her something, but instead began to rummage through her handbag before pulling out a business card of her own. "It's our father's, but I hope it will do."

Ōtani examined the card, then glanced up at the two sisters.

"Is your father the architect Mizuhara? I should have realized."

"Not at all."

Wakako flinched in surprise, lifted the baby into her arms, then jumped to her feet. Her face had turned pale. She began to walk away without so much as a backward glance, tottering on unsteady legs.

The baby was crying.

"Is something wrong?" Momoko asked.

Ōtani, astonished, took off after her.

"What happened?" Momoko looked to Asako. "Could she be going to change the baby's diaper?"

"I wonder . . ."

Ōtani searched the corridor, but there was no sign of either the girl or the baby.

Wakako had left the theater in a daze. She was rushing to tell her mother that she had happened upon her sisters.

By the time she came to, remembering that her mother had gone to the Daitokuji to see her father, she was almost home.

Only then did she awake to the cries of the baby clutched tightly in her arms.

4

The lyrics to the songs of this year's Miyako Odori had been composed by the playwright Yoshii Isamu. The show began with a poem written by the composer: *Joyously do I write the verses of these songs, alive in memory of the elegant Gion of my youth.*"

The show was titled *Mirror of Famous Sights of the Old Capital* and celebrated the most renowned places in the city. Each song was supposed to represent a master of a particular traditional art: "Fresh Verdure of Kamo" recalled the works of the poet Ōtagaki Rengetsu, "Wind on the River in Shijō" paid honor to the technique of kimono dyeing perfected by the painter Miyazaki Yūzen, "Scarlet Kadsura in the Rainy Season" recalled the artworks of the painter Ike no Taiga, "Winter Frost in Shimabara" evoked the tea ceremony as performed by the courtesan Yoshino Tayū, and "Lingering Snow on Takagamine" was dedicated to the calligrapher Hon'ami Kōetsu.

Momoko and Asako were seated near the stage.

Asako spotted Ōtani near the back of the theater. He was alone.

"Mr. Ōtani is sitting by himself. I wonder what happened to the girl."

"She was a strange one. Her face turned deathly pale, as if something had scared her. It was rather rude of her, if you ask me."

"Something must have happened to the baby. She was taking care of her, so she should be with Mr. Ōtani." Asako was worried. "The design of her kimono certainly looked nice, though."

"Ah, so you did notice it?" Momoko answered. "Kyōto kimonos and obis are very fine indeed. She looked like she was around high school age, but I suppose she doesn't go to school."

"Once again, in the twenty-fifth year of this peaceful Shōwa era . . ."

With that announcement began the prelude: "Bamboo Branches East of the Kamo River."

The stage was decorated with silver fusuma panels. Dancers appeared on the two raised *hanamachi* walkways that ran down either side of the theater. As was tradition for the Miyako Odori, each dancer held a fan styled after the branch of a cherry tree.

The thirty-two dancers, sixteen from either side of the theater, approached the stage with slow, leisurely movements.

As their heavily made-up faces drew near, Momoko found herself unsure where to look.

The third act, "Wind on the River in Shijō," and the fifth act, "Winter Frost in Shimabara," were the highlights of the show. In "Winter Frost in Shimabara," the image of the deceased Yoshino appeared to her lover, the merchant Haiya Shōeki, who chased after her in madness. That was the only dramatic dance; yet to Asako, it seemed rather amateurish, leaving her unimpressed.

The Inoue school of Kyōto dance was completely different from the gaudy and lively movements of the Edo style, descended from the tradition of kabuki. It was too refined, too austere; and though she had read all about the Miyako Odori in preparation, she simply couldn't relate to the sluggish tone and pacing. She watched on, despondent.

Perhaps, she wondered, the kabuki stage of the Minamiza was too large for this kind of show?

"So this is the Miyako Odori? I don't see what all the fuss was about. But I suppose it is pretty," she mused, relaxing.

Momoko too looked out of place.

No curtain fell over the stage when the show moved from one scene to the next. The vividly changing backgrounds were like images from a slide projector.

For the final act, "Night Cherries at Maruyama," the dancers paraded down the *hanamachi* walkways once more, holding cherry branches and fans in their hands.

Relieved that the show was finally over, Asako glanced toward her sister. "You look bored."

"It's our fault. We aren't familiar with Kyōto dances, or with the geisha. Maybe if we knew who all the girls were, we would have been able to enjoy it a bit more."

Asako couldn't see Ōtani. Perhaps he had already left the theater?

They stepped outside the building, when they heard a voice. "Miss Mizuhara! Miss Mizuhara!"

Momoko froze.

"How long has it been? It's me, Aoki Natsuji."

"Yes . . ." The color ebbed from Momoko's face.

Seeing her turn pale, the student blushed. "It's been so long," he all but stammered. "My dad . . . well, he said I might find you at your inn, but then I heard you had come to see the Miyako Odori, so I thought I would wait for you out here. It isn't really my thing, and it only goes for around an hour, after all."

"Oh?" Momoko swallowed, fighting to hold back her emotions.

There was a pain digging deep inside her body, a fire burning within her.

A profound sense of shame and anger from her past had come alive once again.

"Natsuji. Was it your father who asked ours to design a tearoom?"

"That's right."

"I see." Momoko turned to her sister with an icy smile. "Father tricked me. I shouldn't have come."

Asako grabbed hold of her sleeve.

"Asako. This is Aoki's brother. Aoki was my . . . lover. He died in Okinawa, in the war."

"Oh dear!"

"Let's walk," Momoko urged.

Shijō was overflowing with people coming out of the theater and with tourists who had come to admire the cherry trees in Maruyama Park.

Asako held on to her sister's arm.

"You were still a child, Asako. You probably didn't realize what was going on," Momoko said softly.

"Yes."

"I wasn't trying to hide it from you, but not even Father really knows."

"My dad and I really are sorry, Momoko," Natsuji said beside them. "He always says how much he wants to apologize to you."

"Oh? But I've nurtured my own sorrow. Your brother simply planted the seed and then flew away. I'm the one who tended to it, who let it sprout." Momoko glanced toward Natsuji. "Are you going to university?"

"I'll graduate next year."

"So soon. In Kyōto?"

"No, in Tōkyō. I'm on vacation."

"So your family has moved here?"

"Yes, but I'm still living in Tōkyō."

At that moment, Asako felt as though she had just seen the young man in a new light.

Her heart was pounding. She realized that she had been staring at him for too long, perhaps trying to find some trace of her sister's deceased lover in his face.

Natsuji told the two sisters that his father had invited them both to dinner.

Momoko nodded. "I'll meet him."

Seeing as they had time, they went to see the flowers in Maruyama Park.

The spring colors of the whole city seem to be brought together in this room, while I lament the fate of the old Maruyama cherry trees . . .

Just as in the song featured in the Miyako Odori, the old weeping cherries had withered and had been replaced by fresh young ones.

They passed by the old Saami restaurant and climbed the slope to the An'yōji Temple. There, they had a full view of Shijō, and beyond it of the hills of Nishiyama veiled in the evening haze.

From their vantage point, Natsuji pointed out one famous sight after another.

Momoko, standing behind him, found her gaze drawn to the back of his neck. It was identical to that of his late brother.

Just looking at his skin, she could sense that he was still a virgin. Her heart aching, she forced her eyes shut. They were wet with tears.

She would have liked to lie in his arms, just once. "How

dull. You're pathetic, you are. Truly pathetic," she would have said, pushing him away. He would struggle, he would cling to her, but still she would avenge herself, doing to him what his brother had done to her.

She trembled with grief, before at last opening her eyes. Braziers had been lit throughout the park to illuminate the cherry blossoms.

The Katsura Imperial Villa

I

An ambulance sped across the busy Maruyama Park, its sirens blaring.

The three of them stopped to ask a passerby what had happened.

"There was a fight. A bunch of folks must have had too much to drink while enjoying the flowers," responded a voice in the Kyōto dialect. "I saw someone lying on the ground, bleeding."

Momoko joked that the stranger who had responded to them sounded remarkably calm, and she and Asako broke out into soft laughter.

Thinking back on it, however, she couldn't help but wonder whether there hadn't been a hint of cruelty in those light Kyōto tones.

But perhaps that was merely a reflection of her own feelings.

She stood watching Natsuji and Asako from behind. Asako didn't particularly resemble her in looks, but Natsuji was almost a mirror image of his brother, Keita. She felt as though she was gazing into her own past, the flames of jealousy licking at her heart.

Natsuji held his school cap in his hand, resting it against his hip. Momoko was sure that the cap had once belonged to Keita. It was a little out of fashion, but seeing as he was still a student, he could probably be excused for wearing it.

She could feel her breasts growing stiff, as though something was pressing up hard against them.

Whatever had happened to that tea bowl?

In truth, it was a stretch to call it a *tea bowl*, but that was how he had always referred to it. It was a silver bowl, she remembered, one that Keita had made using a mold of her breast.

They were kissing that day when he had suggested making it.

He was holding her tightly, his arm circling around her neck, when his hand slipped from her shoulders down to her chest, gently brushing up against her breast.

"No, no." Momoko drew back, covering them with her hands.

"Ah, Mum!" Keita said.

His grip grew more forceful. In her attempt to cover herself, she had merely ended up pushing his hand even farther onto her breast.

"Mum! Ah, Mum!" He groaned again, pulling her closer with his free hand.

"*Mum?*"

His voice seemed to echo through her mind as though from a great distance. She felt her head growing numb. Everything seemed so far away.

"*Mum?*"

It was as though she were calling out for her own mother.

Momoko's strength left her. Keita's free hand circled around her back before coming to a stop as he cupped her breast from above and below.

"Strange . . ." he murmured, pressing his forehead against her chest. "I called you *Mum,* didn't I? It really did feel that way. For a second, I thought I had finally been able to meet her, that I could go to my death with my mind at ease."

Keita too had grown up without a mother. Now, having been drafted into the air force, there was a distinct possibility that death might be just around the corner for him.

Momoko could no longer contain her love.

With her breast having evoked for Keita the image of the mother, she found her sense of modesty abating. She could feel herself drowning in that sacred tenderness.

Moreover, Keita's words had awakened in her a deep-rooted longing for her own mother, whom she had lost while still a child.

"Why am I so calm, I wonder?" he murmured. "I've been so on edge lately, so terrified by the thought of death. But it's all so clear now."

Momoko was fully aware that her chest was uncovered, her breasts exposed.

"Ah . . ."

With a low moan, Keita pressed his forehead between them.

Then, as though to smother his whole face, he put his hands on either side of her breasts, pushing them in.

"Ah!"

Momoko shivered. She tried to leap up from the sofa, but her legs wouldn't move.

She turned pale as though taken by a sudden chill; but almost without realizing it, she found herself grasping his head in her arms. With that, the strange feeling that had overcome her relented.

Keita glanced up at her, his eyes moist. "Momoko, would you let me take a mold of your breast?"

"What?"

She had no idea what he meant.

A mold of her breast, from which he could make a silver tea bowl, he explained.

"I'll use it to drink my last fill of life."

Something in his voice frightened her.

"Long ago, when two people parted ways unsure whether they would ever see each other again, it was normal to share a cup of water. Even today, everyone in the Special Attack Unit drinks a cup of cold saké before going out into battle. So let me make my own final cup. That's how I want to leave this world."

It was an ominous request, but she couldn't refuse him now.

Keita mixed the plaster.

Momoko lay down on the sofa. She closed her eyes to keep her tears from spilling over.

She resisted the first two or three times when he tried to open her collar, but soon resigned herself.

"Beautiful." Keita, standing beside her, paused for a

moment. "I feel like I'm making a sacrifice of you. Maybe we should stop?"

"It's fine. Go on."

He lathered the plaster on her nipple with a bamboo spatula.

"It's cold." Momoko shuddered, pulling in her legs, twisting to one side.

The plaster ran down her breast.

"It tickles! Stop!"

Keita's eyes seemed wild as he stared at her disheveled form.

Momoko frowned and looked up to meet his gaze. She froze, practically pinned down.

She endured that uncomfortable tickling sensation until the blood sapped from her face. Though her eyes were held firmly closed, she could feel his hand trembling.

The sludgy plaster had begun to solidify around her breast.

It felt heavier, as though it were binding her flesh. Painfully so.

She had assumed her breast would contract, but it felt as though it was instead swelling to resist the pressure of the plaster. It grew warm, and that warmth soon spread throughout her body.

She felt suddenly fearless. "Is this how they make death masks?" she murmured.

"Death masks? I suppose it is." But Keita hastened to add, "It might be a death cup, but for me, I plan to drink my last fill of life from it."

Momoko was silent.

Keita smoothed out the plaster with the bamboo spatula.

After waiting for it to harden, he removed it from her breast and stared into it.

"There's a small hollow at the bottom. Your nipple. It's adorable."

"You're embarrassing me. Don't show it to anyone, okay?"

Momoko brought her collar together, sitting up straight.

The cast was smaller, shallower than she had imagined.

"It won't stand upright with the nipple jutting out from the bottom. Maybe I should add some legs?" Keita sank deep into thought for a moment. "How about your little finger? Let me take another mold. Isn't it an old custom to offer your little finger to your beloved?"

And so he applied the plaster to the tip of her finger.

"My dad took an interest in pottery five or six years ago. You know, tea bowls and the like. They weren't very good, of course. But I suppose I have him to thank for this idea."

Momoko turned away, brushing her breast to wipe off the small bits of plaster still stuck to it.

She was so tired. She found herself struck by an ineffable, unbearable sadness.

It was as though, by taking a mold of her breast, he had taken her very life from her.

Perhaps this was to be the end?

She felt unsatisfied. And from the depths of that feeling, a strange ardor began to rise inside her. She wanted to embrace Keita, to hold on to him dearly.

So she didn't resist, not even when he took her in his arms and carried her to the bed in the adjoining room.

"Don't play around anymore," she said, burying her face in his chest.

Keita often enjoyed himself with prostitutes before meeting with her. And what was worse, he told her about it afterward. She couldn't understand why he had to do that.

Why did he need other women? Why did he have to tell her about them?

He said that the prostitutes were true Japanese women, offering themselves to the men of the Special Attack Units. It wasn't unusual for the daughters of the farming villages near the airfield to give themselves to Keita and his fellow airmen either. He recounted these episodes to Momoko too.

He spoke about them lightly, as though they were but mere trifles; yet Momoko could sense his pain and torment. All she could do was forgive him.

Keita respected her purity. He knew that he was destined to die and so was endeavoring not to rob her of her innocence. That she knew.

Perhaps he went to visit those prostitutes before seeing her because he feared his own impulses?

But for her, it was torture. She felt as though she were denying this man, who might die the very next day, the comfort that he so desperately needed.

Keita took from the prostitutes what he should have sought from her.

Why didn't he seek *her* comfort? She was willing to give him everything, without regret.

Wasn't he just trying to wash away the stains of his time with those prostitutes whenever he came to see her?

Momoko wasn't without her doubts. Could Keita's sentimental respect for her purity be nothing but a front, while in his heart, he had repeatedly succumbed to despair, had given himself again and again to momentary dissolution?

Might he not be deceiving himself? Might he not be using her purity as an excuse to justify his self-indulgences? Such doubts were fed by an unspeakable sense of jealousy.

The impetus with which he now moved to take her purity therefore seemed to her as a flash of lightning in the overcast sky of her long love; a radiant, scorching cause for joy.

Keita pulled away.

"Ah," he spat out softly, turning his back to her. "Ah. How dull."

Momoko felt a sudden chill. She lifted herself upright.

Keita, his back still turned to her, stepped out of the bed.

"What was that? You're pathetic. Truly pathetic."

She felt her blood freeze. She couldn't tell whether he was speaking out of hatred or of sadness.

He sat down on the sofa and closed his eyes.

"Break the mold," she all but shouted at him, burning with indignation and anger.

"No."

Keita died without her ever seeing him again.

He must have completed the silver bowl, but he had never shown it to her.

A week later, he was transferred to Kanoya Air Base in southern Kyūshū and met his end in battle in Okinawa.

Five years had passed since then.

Taking a mold of her breast to fashion a silver tea bowl had seemed to her at the time an unreal fantasy, but she knew now that a man and a woman in love were capable of all manner of inexplicable things.

A silver tea bowl in the shape of a breast was, perhaps, a tangible manifestation of his immature sentimentality.

Following behind Natsuji and Asako, faced with their unjaundiced conversation, Momoko found that she couldn't keep watching on in silence.

She drew close to the young man. "Is that your brother's old cap, Natsuji?"

"It is. It was a little small at first, but it fits like a glove now," he replied, glancing back at her.

2

The three of them passed by the great bell of the Chion'in Temple, the largest in all of Japan, and approached the main hall.

Behind the hall, they passed under the Nightingale Hallway, when they found a weeping cherry in full bloom.

Its small pink flowers stood out all the more against the evening haze.

There were no other visitors nearby. The silence was broken only by the distant murmur of activity over in Maruyama Park.

"It's like those withered trees of Gion," Momoko said.

They didn't leave through the colossal main gate, returning instead the way they had come toward Maruyama Park, before entering the Saami.

There, they were led through the garden to a detached room where they found Mizuhara and Keita's father, Aoki.

"Oh, were you waiting for us?" Asako asked.

Natsuji stepped aside to let Momoko pass. As she entered, she greeted Aoki without hesitation.

Aoki stood up from his cushion and welcomed her with a bow.

"Greetings. I've long been hoping to speak with you, Momoko. Thank you for joining us."

"Thank you," she replied, averting her gaze. "But to tell the truth, my father tricked me into coming."

"Yes. He did mention that just now."

Momoko raised her face and stared across at him.

Asako and Natsuji took their seats.

"I see he didn't tell you we had moved to Kyōto either. I thought maybe he would have mentioned it," Aoki said. "Perhaps I shouldn't dredge up something you probably want to leave behind you, something I've long wished to leave in the past, but I'm truly sorry for not letting you know about Keita's death. At the time, I thought it better not to burden you."

"I should be the one to apologize. I never went to express my condolences."

"Not at all. I was waiting for the right time to thank you on his behalf, or rather, to apologize for him. Now that I've had time to reflect on everything, I feel you deserve an apology for the way he died."

"Thank you. I'm sure Momoko understands how you feel," Mizuhara seconded.

"Yes. But I still wanted to offer her my thanks and apologies, to help put the past behind me."

"I haven't forgotten, even if it is passed," Momoko said quietly.

Aoki remained silent for a few moments before confiding, "When Keita died, I realized how much I missed you as well. It was hard not being able to see you."

"I wanted to die too," Momoko said casually. "I took cyanide."

"Momoko?" Asako was dumbfounded.

Mizuhara and Aoki both stared at her.

"It's true," Momoko said to her sister. "At the time, even the girls had all been recruited to the factories. They gave us each a dose in case we got badly injured in an air raid, or if the enemy came ashore. Each of us had one, remember? I took mine."

"Wh-when?"

"But it was only sugar."

"Sugar?"

"I really did think it was cyanide. But someone had changed its contents without my knowing. The second I put it in my mouth, the second I tasted that sweetness, I knew Mother was responsible. She saved my life."

Asako stared at her in disbelief.

"I'm grateful to her. But it's a curious thing, this human life. I only survived because she swapped my cyanide with sugar. I haven't sought death again since then. Thanks to her concern for me, she saved my life, without even realizing it. When I tasted that sugar, I started thinking about my own mother's suicide. I was terrified."

Momoko's confession had chilled the room.

Asako was stunned. "I . . . I had no idea . . ."

"It isn't the kind of thing you tell people, that you took sugar thinking it was cyanide. Maybe not even Mother knew I took it, meaning to kill myself. But I'm grateful to her."

Asako couldn't understand why her sister was mentioning this all now.

Nor was she entirely convinced that she was telling the whole truth.

It was possible that Natsuji and his father were aware that Momoko's birth mother had ended her own life. But why, Asako wondered, had her sister chosen to reveal this fact here?

Dinner was served, but the conversation had fallen silent.

From their dining room, they had a night view of the city very similar to that which they had enjoyed from the nearby An'yōji a short time earlier. They could even make out the braziers illuminating the trees in Maruyama Park.

Aoki was two or three years older than Mizuhara, but he looked the younger of the two.

He had a handsome forehead, and his eyes glimmered with vitality. His plump hands seemed unsuited to his face.

Those hands were just like Keita's.

Not even Natsuji's cheeks were as warm as his father's. Aoki's blood may have been that of an older man, but it flowed with youthful vigor.

Momoko, already struggling with memories of Keita, found herself growing weak at the sight of his father.

3

The entrance permit to the Katsura Imperial Villa listed the names of Mizuhara, Momoko, Asako, and Natsuji, but both Mizuhara and Momoko had decided not to go.

Given his renown as an architect, Mizuhara's name might

have been meant simply to gain them entrance, but Momo-ko's absence came as a surprise to Asako.

When Natsuji arrived at their inn at Sanjō, Momoko had already gone out.

"She went to the station to meet someone coming from Tōkyō," Asako said, her cheeks turning red.

The Takemiya boy had followed her all the way to Kyōto, it seemed.

"And your father?"

"He went to Nara. They're both out enjoying themselves." She found herself echoing what Momoko had said the other day.

They changed trains at Shijō-Ōmiya and got off at Katsura Station.

To reach the villa, they had to walk back part of the way toward the Katsura River.

"Maybe we should have come by bus? We could have gotten off by the river and followed the bamboo wall right to the entrance," Natsuji observed.

But for Asako, their stroll through the wheat fields came as an unexpected joy. There were fields of rapeseed too. Hearing the unusual cry of a skylark, she stared up into the sky.

They were in one of the most open areas in Kyōto, and the view extended from the nearby Mount Arashiyama to Mount Atago past Mount Ogura, all the way to the distant Mount Hiei and Kitayama. Higashiyama was shrouded in mist.

Asako glanced around, taking in the spring landscape.

"I wish Momoko could have come."

"That night after coming home from the Saami, my dad and I spoke a lot about what she said," Natsuji remarked.

Asako glanced around. "What did you say?"

"I was struck by how something as small as changing the contents of a cyanide capsule with sugar could have such a profound impact on someone's life, and what might have happened if your mother hadn't done it."

"But I'm not really sure she truly did take it."

"It's an interesting story, even if it was made up. But I think she was telling the truth."

"No one at home knew anything."

"Your mother was a wise woman."

"I'm sure any parent would have done the same if their child had brought something so dangerous home."

"It would be no good just hiding it away. They might get their hands on another." Natsuji paused for a moment. "But my brother always kept his own cyanide in his desk drawer. Right up until our house was destroyed. When your sister was telling us about what happened, I feared at first he had given his to her."

Asako was shaken.

"And I wondered whether she was telling us it all now to spite how we handled everything after his death."

"I'm sure that wasn't it."

"Anyway, as she said, life is a curious thing. These kinds of situations really do happen. Last night, it struck me that she was only alive today because she had taken sugar instead of poison, and she seemed all the more beautiful for that."

They passed through an area laid out like a small hamlet. Kerria flowers were blooming amid cracks in the decaying plaster walls of the buildings.

"Apparently, my brother burned his diaries and letters before he died. He didn't leave anything for us to remember him by. All we got back from his unit was some sort of silver bowl."

"She said not even our father really knew about her relationship with your brother."

"Yes. But my dad told me he would like Momoko to come stay with us for a while. He suggested as much to your father."

Perhaps, Asako thought, her father wanted to entrust Momoko to the Aoki family for a time to help her find a sense of healing?

The two of them arrived in front of the villa.

On the lawn in front of the gate, in the shadows of the pine trees, dandelions and lotuses were in bloom. A double-flowered camellia had blossomed in front of the bamboo fence.

The Bridge of Life

I

The Katsura Imperial Villa was surrounded by a bamboo hedge that could easily have been mistaken for a natural grove.

Toward the entrance, however, was a fence made from woven bamboo grass.

As the main gate was reserved for imperial visits, regular visitors approached through the entrance to the right.

Asako showed her permit at the guard post.

"Miss Mizuhara?" the guard asked before turning to Natsuji. "You aren't wearing spiked shoes, are you?"

"No," Natsuji replied, showing one of his soles.

After passing the guard post, they entered the waiting room set aside for visitors.

Natsuji sat down on an old chair. "Do they really think students are going to wreck the gardens by wearing spiked shoes? Even we have enough sense not to do that."

"Yes. But I heard some of the stone pavements and ornamental rocks have been damaged by visitors," Asako said. "Even rocks get worn out when people walk on them every day."

"I see. So it's to stop everyday wear and tear."

"My father told me that even today, with admission much easier than it was before the war, the number of visitors allowed in each day is strictly limited. And the buildings are probably more at risk now too. They were built three hundred years ago, in a simple style modeled on Zen monastic dwellings. Not only that, they were designed as residences and weren't built to cater to so many visitors. No more than fifteen people are allowed to enter at a time, because their weight could damage the corridors."

Tours were scheduled for several times throughout the day, and visitors were supposed to stay in the waiting room until a caretaker came to meet them.

Asako, however, following her father's advice, went back to the guard post and asked for permission to wander the grounds without a guide.

"You're Mr. Mizuhara's daughter? Very well. Please, go ahead."

And so the two of them began to stroll through the gardens.

When they came to a small gate with a thatched roof, they spied beyond it the famous stone path with its large, almost regular flagstones, and so decided to take a look.

Across from the path was the palanquin staging area. At either side of the pavement were ornamental stones covered in thick green moss.

"The haircap moss is flowering!" they said in unison, before meeting each other's gaze.

The stems were thinner than silken threads, almost invisible to the eye. They were like little naked stamens floating just above the green sheet of moss.

The flowers looked to be frozen in place; but on closer inspection, Asako could see that they were swaying almost imperceptibly from side to side.

They had both been struck by the subtle beauty of those small flowers, expressing their amazement almost at the exact same moment.

No words, however, could be enough to describe that sense of beauty. They had merely communicated what they had seen, their voices carrying all the emotion that came with that sight.

The architect Bruno Taut once described the Katsura Imperial Villa as the ultimate embodiment of Japanese architecture, writing that the source of its subtle art could be found in meditation, contemplation, and Zen philosophy. The moss flowers in bloom by the entrance certainly lent themselves to that gentle impression.

They evoked also the tender image of spring.

Asako and Natsuji followed the path to the palanquin staging area, and from there to the entrance of the main building with its three adjoining halls, built in stages over the course of the seventeenth century. At the top of the steps was a stone slab where visitors were expected to remove their footwear: the Sixfold Stepping Stone, given its name as it was large enough to accommodate six pairs of shoes.

Here, the walls of the building were painted with red

ocher, as was the custom in Kyōto. The dividing walls demarcating the inner garden were of the same color.

Past the wall was the Moon Wave Pavilion, but the pair returned to the main path and entered a garden overlooking a maple hillock.

"To think you can find cycads here of all places!" Natsuji exclaimed.

"They were a gift from the Shimazu clan," Asako explained. "They're a little out of place, but they must have been a rare sight back when they were planted."

Natsuji entered the small pavilion opposite and sat down. Asako remained standing.

It had come as a surprise to find more than a dozen cycads as far north as Kyōto. Nonetheless, those tropical plants seemed strangely appropriate in the shade of the luxuriant Japanese trees and lent a fresh touch to the path leading to the tearoom.

Natsuji removed his cap and placed it on his knees. "It's nice and quiet. Can you hear the water?"

"It's probably the Hand Drum Waterfall. The sound must be from the chute bringing water into the pond from the Katsura River."

"You're very knowledgeable about all this, Asako."

"I read a guidebook earlier."

"I read Bruno Taut's book on the Katsura Imperial Villa back when I was in high school, but I don't remember it very well."

"It would be nice if Father were here with us."

"Yes. But I'm sure he must already be quite familiar with all this. Your sister should have joined us, though."

Asako wondered what exactly Natsuji meant by that. His words made her acutely aware that the two of them had come alone.

"Can you hear it?" she asked to break the silence. "The skylark is back."

"The same one from the path?" Natsuji turned toward the sound. "It does sound like a skylark, but there's no way of knowing whether it's the same one we saw in the wheat fields. There must be a lot of them around here."

"It's the same one. I'm sure of it."

"Is that your feminine intuition speaking? Your sister certainly has a sixth sense. She knew this cap used to belong to my brother the moment she saw it. I mean, these student caps all look the same. Frankly, I'm amazed she knew it used to be his."

"But there weren't any other skylarks."

"Sure there are," Natsuji insisted. "Your sister was staring at me like she was looking for similarities between me and my brother. My eyes, my ears, my shoulders, that kind of thing. It made me feel a little uneasy."

"It does sound uncomfortable. But isn't it a good thing you resemble him? For her?"

"Why do you say that?"

"Because it must comfort her."

"Oh? I would have thought the opposite. Wouldn't it be better for her to come see this villa with us, rather than look for my brother in me? Even if my brother wore this cap back when the two of them were together, is there anything left from that time in it now?" Natsuji clutched the cap in his hand as he rose to his feet.

"Maybe I'm the opposite of my sister. When I see you, I try to imagine what your brother must have looked like. I never knew him."

"That makes me feel uncomfortable too. Anyway, I'm not my brother's shadow. Our personalities are completely different."

"Yes."

"And our destinies too. Here with you now, Asako, it isn't your sister's face that comes to mind for me."

"That's because we don't look at all alike," she responded lightly, blushing. "Besides, she and I are both still alive."

"Yes. My brother departed this world without leaving anything to remember him by. And because of that, everything reminds us of him. After he died, I blamed my dad. I told him he was being selfish, wanting to meet Momoko. I said he was only trying to remember his dead son, trying to indulge his own grief by seeing her. Even if Momoko mourns Keita too, I'm sure their feelings must be quite different by now."

Asako nodded. "But still . . ."

"Maybe this isn't for me to say, but don't you think there might still be a bridge between my dead brother and your living sister?"

"I wouldn't know. But I'm sure there must be."

If there was such a bridge, Asako suspected that it would be rotten and decayed, far too dangerous for anyone to dare to cross. Perhaps Momoko had been the first to fall from it?

"But I suspect there's no shore on the other side. Even if someone still living tried to cross it, it would just stretch out into the void. No matter how far you go, you wouldn't reach anywhere."

"Are you saying that if someone you love dies, then the love you share with them dies too?"

"I'm speaking from the point of view of the living. From Momoko's perspective."

"I don't believe in heaven or paradise, but I do want to believe in memories of love for those who have passed."

"Yes. As long as those memories are quiet and peaceful, like the villa here, and don't inflict further pain on the living."

"Yes. Even if Momoko had joined us, with you here, Natsuji, I'm sure she would just end up thinking about your brother."

"Anyway, he's dead. He can't enjoy this garden with us. But we're still alive, and today, we can see it. And if we wanted to come back tomorrow, we could see it then too. Let's leave it at that."

"Yes."

"It's like they say: *The beauty of a single flower is enough to reawaken one's will to live.*"

"But I wonder why Momoko never mentioned what happened between herself and your brother to my father or me?"

"Maybe she always knew it was an impossible love? That it would end in tragedy?"

"Do you think so?" Asako looked to Natsuji.

"I do. From what I can see, their love only truly blossomed when Momoko realized my brother was certain to die in the war."

"Do you really think so?" she asked again.

"But it's strange, isn't it? We've come all the way to see the villa here, and all we've done is talk about my brother and your sister." Natsuji smiled.

"It is, isn't it?" Asako too found herself smiling. "I wonder why?"

2

The pond unfolded before them as they left the pavilion and crossed the stream.

"That sound just before must have been the Hand Drum Waterfall," Natsuji said.

"Yes. It said in the guidebook that the water used to be clearer and sounded just like a real waterfall as it entered the pond. It must have been less stagnant then," Asako replied.

Natsuji approached the water's edge.

The Bridge of Heaven, a path modeled after the famous pine-covered sandbar spanning the mouth of Miyazu Bay, extended out into the pond. There was a stone lantern at the end of the path, and on the opposite side of the pond stood the Pine Lute Pavilion, the main tearoom.

The landscape was said to evoke the impression of a beach.

An old woman was picking grasses sprouting from between the small stones that paved the Bridge of Heaven.

Natsuji stopped next to her and watched for a short moment before asking, "Do you come here every day, ma'am?"

"Oh yes. Every day."

"How many of you are there?"

"Picking the grass? Just the two of us."

"Only two?"

"Two pairs of hands aren't enough, of course. The garden alone is more than ten acres in size. We only really work on the pathways."

"How much do you earn?"

The old woman didn't respond. Natsuji repeated the question.

"Only a trifle, I'm ashamed to say."

"Two hundred yen a day, maybe?"

"Oh, that would be nice," the woman murmured. "Around half that."

"A hundred yen?"

"A little more. Add another twenty."

"A hundred and twenty yen?"

The woman continued to pick at the grasses without looking up.

"That's more than the old women who carry cedar logs in Takao," Asako said.

She found herself recounting how, shortly after arriving in Kyōto, her father had taken her to Takao to see the fresh leaves of the maple trees at what was said to be the best time of year.

They had descended Mount Takao from the Jingoji Temple, crossed the river that flowed into the valley, and made their way halfway up another steep slope before coming across a group of women who had stopped to take a break from hauling several thick cedar logs down the mountain. One of the women looked to be around fifteen or sixteen years of age, another perhaps twenty, while the remaining four seemed to be in their fifties. The younger girls must have been apprentices, as they were carrying the smallest log between them.

While Asako and her father stopped to catch their breath and rest their legs, the women all rose to their feet and placed the heavy logs on their heads. Given how long and heavy the cedar logs were, it took the women a little time to get them into position. It didn't look easy.

With a bitter smile, one of the older women revealed

that they made a hundred yen for carrying that load up and down the valley from the mountain to the village three times a day. They could hardly muster their strength living off rationed rice gruel, she complained.

"That mustn't be easy," the old gardener said after listening to Asako's story, before looking up for the first time. "But even if the work is harder, it must be shorter too."

"Really?"

"Their backs were straight, no?"

"They were carrying the logs on their heads, so they had good postures."

"I'm sure. There's nothing to be done for someone bent like me."

Asako and Natsuji retraced their steps on the Bridge of Heaven and followed the path into a grove.

There were camellia petals strewn over the moss and bamboo stems peeking out through gaps in the thick foliage.

"There was a hymn recital competition when we went to the Jingoji," Asako said. "Lots of people came from all over the countryside to take part. They were all gathered in the main hall, and the monks were judging the performances. It was fun. They even rang the bells just like in the Amateur Singing Contest on the radio."

"That does sound fun."

"It was different from the Amateur Singing Contest, though," Asako continued. "We went there to see the statue of the Medicine Buddha, but the main hall was crowded with people taking part in the competition. The songs sounded better from a little distance away. They were local songs, the kind that call to mind a distant hometown. It was a competition, so the singers were very good. Listening to them from under the towering maple trees, I thought to myself that *this* was the real Kyōto."

The young maple leaves set against the wide blue sky had suggested a quintessentially Japanese pattern. Asako could vividly recall the brilliant light of that late-spring afternoon.

"It's true. Pilgrims in this part of the country are known for their hymns," Natsuji said.

"They're very nostalgic," Asako replied.

"But in this religious city, both the mayor and the governor belong to the Socialist Party," Natsuji continued. "Since you arrived here, the candidate from the Socialist Party won in the gubernatorial election. I saw in the newspaper that the new governor was greeted by members of the Communist Party and trade unionists all waving their red flags. And it sounds like both he and the mayor are going to be at the forefront of the parade at this year's May Day. There's another side to Kyōto, distinct from the Katsura Imperial Villa and those Buddhist hymns."

"We're like tourists here."

"My family might be based here now, but when it comes to this city, I'm still a tourist too, wanting to hear those hymns."

"It's natural to feel nostalgic for things like that."

"Did your sister go with you to Takao?"

"Yes. She was the one who was most absorbed in the songs."

"I see," Natsuji answered. "But it looks like we've found ourselves talking about her again."

Didn't they have any other topics worth discussing? Or was it perhaps difficult for them to bring up anything else?

They climbed a small hill and came to a rest house formerly used during breaks in the tea ceremony.

There were four benches arranged in a pattern so that even if they were all occupied, no one would be directly facing anyone else. The building was famed for its expert use of rotational symmetry.

Anyone who entered could talk without looking directly at anyone else's face, or they could choose to sit in silence.

Asako and Natsuji remained quiet for a short while.

All of a sudden, she remembered a line from the English poet William Blake: *Love that never told can be.*

Asako didn't believe in that kind of sentiment.

She had yet to experience such pain from love that might prompt her to fully accept it.

Nonetheless, the words were unforgettable and had been engraved deep in her heart.

Sitting among the quiet trees, they sounded in her mind almost as prophecy.

She found herself unable to bear the silence any longer.

"I can't hear the skylark anymore," she said.

"You're right." Natsuji leaned forward, straining his ears. "The trees are blocking the view from here. I wonder whether it was designed like this when it was first built, or whether it was once possible to make out the garden, the pond, the main building, and even the hills of Nishiyama off into the distance. Trees grow and wither, so it's dangerous to think the garden still looks just as it did several hundred years ago. But at least we can see some of the remaining cherry blossoms through the trees. There were three or four cherry trees by the New Hall, weren't there? They should plant more."

"Yes." Asako had seen them too. "The day we arrived in Kyōto, my father went to the Daitokuji to meet a monk. He said there were no cherry trees on the grounds. He didn't think to mention it at the time, but he told me it reminded him of the biography of the monk-painter Minchō in *The History of Japanese Painting*."

"I've read *The History of Japanese Painting*, but I can't remember any of it."

"The shōgun Yoshimochi was particularly fond of Minchō's work and offered to grant him anything he wanted. Minchō wasn't interested in money or rank, but he did have one request. At the time, the monks at the Tōfukuji Temple had planted a great many cherry trees on the grounds, but Minchō was afraid those cherries would one day transform the temple into a place of frivolity and entertainment. So he asked the shōgun to remove them. The shōgun agreed, and had all the trees cut down."

"Oh? Minchō had a very rough style, so I can imagine that. But now with the war over, so many temples have been turned into clandestine restaurants anyway, even letting geisha and *maiko* in." Natsuji rose to his feet.

Asako removed a mirror from her purse and began to tidy her hair.

The Silver Breast

I

After descending the hill from the rest house and crossing a large stone bridge, Asako and Natsuji came to the Pine Lute Pavilion.

The bridge was comprised of a single piece of Shirakawa stone more than five meters long and so was called the Shirakawa Bridge. It was said to have been presented as a gift by the feudal lord Katō Samanosuke.

Natsuji paused atop it, with Asako quickly following suit.

He wanted to ask her to stay where she was for a moment so that he could contemplate her figure atop the bridge, but he didn't dare express that wish.

"Being surrounded by all these rocks makes your heart feel pretty heavy, don't you think?" he said.

"It does, doesn't it?" Asako responded vaguely.

"I don't know much about rock arrangements. I wonder if this is the kind of design Kobori Enshū was known for?"

"I wouldn't know."

"There must have been a lot of attention paid to the rock arrangements around here. I don't know if you could call it severe or poignant, but if you ask me, this kind of obsessive attention to detail has to be due to a nervous temperament. Just standing here, it's like these stones are all grating against my nerves. They're so craggy and sharp."

"They're just rocks," Asako said lightly.

"No, they're more than that. They're laid out this way to express something. Maybe it's because people like you and me can't imagine what it means to create beauty simply by positioning natural rocks on top of natural ground, but these arrangements, supposed to be so rich in meaning, just end up feeling so suffocating. People like us don't have an eye for garden aesthetics. But I suppose that applies to a lot of gardens, not just this one. Maybe this one is just a little more overwrought than usual."

"Don't you think you might be paying too much attention to the rock arrangements?"

Natsuji glanced back at Asako. "The moment I stood on this stone bridge and saw the rocks laid out around us, I was struck by a feeling that we shouldn't cross to the other side. And I wondered just who would look most natural standing on this bridge in the middle of this rock arrangement."

"That would be Prince Katsura, wouldn't it?"

"Maybe someone from the prince's era? But then I thought the person who I most wanted to see standing on it was you, Asako."

"Oh?" Blushing, she tried to conceal herself behind Natsuji's back.

"I really did think so," he insisted.

"But why? You're embarrassing me."

"And then it occurred to me that these aren't just stones."

"They aren't?"

"We were talking about the bridge earlier. The bridge between my dead brother and your sister?"

"Yes."

"That was a formless bridge, a bridge of the heart, I suppose you could say; but this, this is a bridge of stone, a bridge of beauty, one that has been standing here for more than three hundred years. If this kind of bridge could exist between two souls . . ."

"A bridge of stone? Wouldn't that be awful, building a stone bridge over your heart? I would prefer a rainbow bridge."

"Well, a bridge between two souls might well be a rainbow, yes."

"But this stone bridge might also be linking two hearts, you know?"

"You may be right. It *was* built as an expression of art and beauty."

"Yes. They say Prince Toshihito, the first Prince Katsura, read from *The Tale of Genji* every day and loved it so much he had this villa modeled on it. The area around the Pine Lute Pavilion is supposed to resemble Akashi Bay."

"It doesn't look much like the coast at Akashi, though, what with all those weird craggy rocks."

"That's what it says in the guidebook. And since Prince Toshihito's wife was born in Tango Province, he modeled this on the Bridge of Heaven there."

Natsuji glanced over at the strip of land as he crossed the stone bridge.

They stepped under the deep eaves of the Pine Lute Pavilion and entered the main building through the Second Room.

There, they sat down and gazed for a time at the rocks near the bridge.

Next, they went to the adjoining tearoom, where they sat for a time too.

After the tearoom, they passed again through the Second Room as they entered the First Room.

The floor and walls from the tokonoma alcove to the fusuma panels were covered in a checkered green-and-blue mulberry design combined with a Kaga votive calligraphy, a renowned, bold display of ingenuity, flamboyant and eccentric in such a sober environment.

Next, the two visitors stepped onto a protruding covered veranda, where the charcoal stove and the shelves for the tea ceremony utensils were installed, and sat in silence.

The pond wrapped around the Pine Lute Pavilion from right to left.

However, both sides looked different when viewed from the First Room.

On the right side, past the shelves for the tea utensils, the arrangement of the rocks next to the stone bridge stood out even more than the water itself; while on the left, the pond in the direction of Hotarudani was deep and stagnant, and the fact that the stones were hidden from sight made the surface seem all the vaster.

Natsuji wondered whether the grating design of the rock arrangement in the one part of the garden contributed to making the overall landscape seem more tightly defined, but he couldn't tell for sure.

"It's kind of strange, being here like this, don't you think?" he said.

Asako stared across the pond to avoid meeting his gaze.

To either side of the tall cedars were the Old Hall and the Moon Wave Pavilion.

The branches of those cedars had withered with the passing of the seasons, but the hedge in front of the Moon Wave Pavilion was lush with young, tender leaves.

2

Since returning to Tōkyō, Asako's impressions of the Katsura Imperial Villa had only grown stronger.

That was partly because she had spoken to her father about her visit and learned about all the qualities for which it was so renowned.

She had also retrieved all the reference texts and photo books that discussed the villa from his bookshelf, piling them up on her desk.

She read through each and every one of them.

That was a characteristic trait of hers. After visiting the Hōryūji Temple in Nara, for example, she greedily devoured as many books as she could find about it. It was the same with music. Once, returning home after listening to a Mozart performance, she had lost herself in research on the European composer.

"There's no point reading so much about it now. You should have prepared beforehand. Knowing you, you'll probably hire someone to investigate your boyfriend's background only after you end up marrying him," Momoko joked.

Her father, however, had a great fondness for Asako's sense of drive and focus, also attributing to this the surprising extent to which she was able to reproduce at home rare dishes that they had enjoyed at restaurants.

It was this habit of hers that prompted her to consume every piece of information that she could find about the Katsura Imperial Villa.

Momoko, however, viewed her relentless reading through a lens of doubt.

Asako showed her sister a photograph of the First Room in the New Hall, pointing to the elevated stage where the most senior guests and their retinues would sit. "I sat in here for a few minutes too."

"Oh? With Natsuji?"

But Asako didn't notice the sarcasm in her sister's voice. "No, he didn't come in. I sat with my legs hanging over the edge beneath the window here, to look out onto the garden."

The First Room was nine tatami mats in size, with the elevated stage comprising a third of that area. The coffered ceiling hung lower above the stage than it did the rest of the room. On the back wall were the famous Katsura Shelves, a staggered group of ornamental brackets renowned as one of the Three Unrivaled Shelves of Old Kyōto.

The upper part of the room was modeled after an extended tokonoma alcove, Asako explained.

A single piece of Karakuwa wood fitted close to the floor

in front of the window served as a reading desk. Beneath the desk was another small window that could be opened during the summer to let in a cool breeze.

Asako had sat at that desk, opening the shōji screen at the window from the inside while Natsuji opened the door from the outside.

The young leaves of the garden flowed into her field of vision. The trees, however, were far from the window, the view a little too bright and sparse.

"Don't you think it's strange, looking at a photograph like this and remembering how I sat right here?" Asako asked her sister.

"I suppose so," Momoko answered vaguely. "But you're not in the photo there."

"Of course not!" Asako laughed. "What are you saying? You should have come with us."

Though she seldom used it, Momoko was sitting in front of the sewing machine.

Asako rose to her feet and glanced at the photographs next to the machine.

"But you know, even after we went to the Katsura Imperial Villa, you were all that Natsuji and I could talk about."

"Me?"

"Yes, and his brother too."

"Oh?" Momoko responded coldly. "I should have guessed. How mortifying."

"We didn't say anything bad, not about you or Keita."

"That's what's so unpleasant about it. You would have acted like the attentive, loving sister you are and said only nice things."

"You're awful."

"And Natsuji, I'm sure, must have spoken well about Keita too."

"Of course."

"You can both say what you like, but if you were trying to get to the truth, you failed."

"We weren't pretending to know what happened, or to understand how you felt."

"I wonder." Momoko slammed her foot down on the sewing machine pedal, then took the sleeves of the dress that she was adjusting and threw them over the photograph. "If you're going to talk about me with Natsuji, you could at least do so with a cool head, like you would if you were speaking about a stranger. I don't appreciate your sympathy. I don't need you to act like you understand."

Asako stared at her sister's hands in silence as they moved about her sewing.

"What you think you understand is nothing more than your own imaginings." Momoko pressed her trembling fingertips against the fabric. "I can only guess what you said, but I'm sure you spoke to Natsuji in the same tone you use when you're talking about me with Father."

"Momoko!"

"What? Only your tears will make me stop now, Asako. There's nothing wrong with being kind, but there are times when a woman's kindness can be entirely self-indulgent. Your kindness is directed only at yourself. Even when you're trying to soothe Father and me, acting like you're trying to save us."

"To save you? I've never thought like that."

"But you've certainly saved Father. He's a decent man. Maybe it's strange for a daughter to say that about her own father, and yet . . ."

"It's true."

"I'm cynical, twisted. He, on the other hand, is so pure that no one seeking your hand in marriage would ever be good enough for him."

Asako was taken aback.

"A father like that will never be able to help his daughter's feelings mature. You shouldn't spend so much time with him, indulging your kindness. It won't be long before you realize the gentler a woman's soul, the greater the depths of pain and suffering she falls into." Momoko stopped the machine for a moment. "Do you think I'm saying this out of jealousy?"

Asako, staring down at her sister's hair, shook her head.

Momoko continued her sewing. "I'm terribly jealous, actually. I don't know what you and Natsuji said about Keita and me at the villa. But lately, I've started to think I shouldn't have let him go off to die in the war. It would have been better if I had killed him myself."

To Asako, that sounded like an expression of love for Keita.

Yet Momoko continued, "Not because I still love him. Because I hate him."

Asako didn't dare respond.

"And my mother too; rather than ending her own life, she should have killed Father. No one should have to die just because they can't marry someone. They would be better off killing them instead. You should keep that in mind too, Asako."

"What has come over you, Momoko?"

"It's the strangest thing. If my mother had killed Father, you would never have been born. Would you? And it would have been the same outcome if my mother had married him instead. It makes you wonder."

Asako shuddered.

It was true, she realized; if Momoko's mother hadn't ended her own life and had instead married their father, she would most likely never have been born. But why was Momoko coming out with all these horrible thoughts?

Was she spitting out the arrows of hatred and resentment that had long poisoned her heart?

Asako felt as though she had been cast down upon a cold, hard surface.

She couldn't understand why her sister was so angry that she had spoken with Keita's brother.

She left Momoko's side and sat down on her bed.

They shared a large Western-style room on the second floor of the house, around ten tatami mats in size, filled with furniture ranging from a mirror to the sewing machine.

"Good night, Asako. Am I bothering you?" Momoko asked. "I'm almost done. I've already attached one sleeve."

Asako slowly let her hand fall to the bedsheet.

"You're inviting Natsuji over next Sunday, aren't you? Because of how nice he and his father were to us in Kyōto? Just so you know, I won't be home. I wouldn't be able to stand it. It's humiliating for me just to be around him. Apparently, Father told Mr. Aoki about our Kyōto sister when he paid him a visit. But still he won't say anything to us. He didn't even mention her to you, did he?" Hammering the pedal of the sewing machine, without waiting for Asako to respond, she continued, "When I heard, I wished I had never gone to Kyōto. We were supposed to be visiting as a family, but we all ended up going our separate ways. Father didn't tell you, did he, that he mentioned how considerate you are to a friend of his? Not just toward him and me, but to our Kyōto sister too? No, I don't want to see Natsuji here, not in this house. You probably think I'm saying this out of concern for Father, but I'm not. It's jealousy, that's all. I may doubt love, but I don't doubt jealousy."

Her heart panged, yet Asako felt as though she had caught the faintest glimpse of her sister's innermost feelings.

She changed into her nightgown and lay down.

As she closed her eyes, she remembered her sister's cruel words.

But she didn't cry.

"Good night," she said.

Momoko had scolded her, claiming that she was always trying to soothe and help both her and her father. Yet Asako couldn't help but wonder whether that charge was really true.

When Momoko finished attaching the remaining sleeve of her dress, she approached her sister's bed and stared down at her in silence for a long moment.

Asako waited for her to say something before opening her eyes, but Momoko remained silent.

Eventually, she made her way downstairs, retrieving a bottle of their father's wine.

Then, she pulled a silver tea bowl from her chest of drawers and poured herself a glass.

She began to take a drink, when she startled and moved to switch off the light.

The moment the room fell dark, Asako burst into tears.

"So you were awake?" Momoko said quietly. "This is why I hate you."

"Momoko, why? Why are you always so mean to me?"

"I suppose I must be jealous, no? That has to be it." She gulped down her drink in the darkness. "I need a little medicine to help me fall asleep."

3

Just as she had warned her sister, when Natsuji came to visit, Momoko fled to Hakone with the Takemiya boy.

From Tōkyō, they boarded a tourist bus that would take them deep into the mountains.

Momoko closed her eyes, but no sooner did the bus pass through Yokohama than the scent of wheat fields wafted in through the window.

"These pines used to line the old Tōkaidō highway, right?" the boy asked her.

The early-morning sun shone in through the window, the shadows of the pine trees flashing across his cheeks.

Momoko opened her eyes. "Don't talk like that. You sound like a girl."

"Do you remember when you made me sing with you? Because you said I had a girl's voice?"

"Yes. It was on a snowy day, on the shore of Lake Ashi."

"It was a blizzard."

"We took a boat across the lake before it started snowing."

"I had so much fun. Even when the bus got stuck on the

mountain on the way home." The boy took Momoko's hand, placed it in his lap, and traced her palm with his finger.

"You're cold. Your hands are always warm in the winter and cool in the summer. I like them."

To Momoko, it seemed as though the boy was caressing not just her hands but her entire body. "Oh?"

"Are all women like this?" he asked from his seat beside the window.

The wide trunks of the pine trees sped past outside.

Since it was a weekday, the bus was almost empty.

As they crossed over the Banyū River, they saw a flock of birds gathered on the railway bridge.

After passing Yumoto and reaching Mount Hakone, Momoko retrieved a gold necklace from her handbag and hooked it around her neck.

The front of the necklace reached the small bulge at the top of her ribs.

She barely spoke to Takemiya, merely offering vague responses to his attempts at conversation.

They stepped off the bus at Hakone and went straight to the hotel across the road.

She had been meaning to stay here tonight, but instead of asking for a room, she made her way into the lounge and sat down by the window.

"What should we do?" she asked Takemiya. "Maybe we could go farther out across the lake?"

"If you want to. Are you tired from the bus trip?"

"It's because I'm so tired that I want to keep going. I thought we could stay here, but it looks like they're doing some renovation work. This isn't at all what I wanted."

Construction to extend the building into the garden overlooking the lake was underway, with the new foundations already in place. If they stayed here, she would no doubt be woken in the morning by the sound of workers preparing reinforced concrete. That prospect, however, was somehow comforting.

Nonetheless, they decided to take the two o'clock boat to the far shore of the lake. As they had time to wait, they ate lunch at the hotel.

The pleasure boat was crowded with passengers from Moto-Hakone, and most of the seats on the deck were full.

There was a mountain lodge toward the shore on their right, Takemiya pointed out. "The greenery must be so beautiful at this time of year."

"We had our fill of greenery in Kyōto. Don't you remember the beech trees and the flowers at Higashiyama?"

"No. I only had eyes for you, Momoko."

"You're a good liar. I taught you to tell the difference between beech and chestnut trees by smell, didn't I?"

"I'm not paying attention to Lake Ashi now, either."

Small waves shone on the surface of the water. Looking closer, she could see that while the waves in the wake of the boat were gleaming in the light, those in front of it were a deep blue in color, probably as the vessel was moving in the direction of the afternoon sun.

Those low waves, like a shimmering fire in the auburn light, widened as they approached the southern shore.

Only the summit of Mount Fuji beyond the bow of the boat was hidden behind a veil of white clouds.

The bus from Kojiri to Mount Sōun was crowded with passengers from the boat; so much so that even though Momoko was fortunate enough to get a seat, she couldn't raise her head without bumping into the people surrounding her.

Only when the bus reached the crater of Ōwakudani was she able to turn her head and catch a glimpse of the lake. The bus seemed to graze the edges of the dense forest as it traversed the winding road. Takemiya reached out from the window, plucking a handful of flowering leaves from the long branches.

At Mount Sōun, they took the cable car to Gōra.

The boy brought the flowers to their room at the inn and placed them on the table. "Momoko," he murmured, pulling at her necklace.

"That hurts. You're hurting me."

"You forgot about me, didn't you?"

Momoko tried to undo the clasp.

"No, leave it on . . . I won't pull on it anymore. It looks good on you, so leave it on."

"If you like it so much, Little Miya . . ." she began, before finding herself feeling somehow disappointed that the boy was so attracted to it.

Nonetheless, she continued to wear it, even while taking a bath in the hot spring and when she settled into her pillow.

As soon as they lay down, the boy grabbed the necklace between his teeth.

"Little Miya's shiny toy," Momoko said.

The boy, still tugging the necklace with his teeth, pressed his face against her neck and began to cry.

She felt tickled. "Enough with this playacting. It's unseemly."

"You're going to abandon me, aren't you?"

"This again? Stop it. At the very least, say that we'll be *parting ways*."

"It's the same thing. I don't care what you call it."

"But you're so morbid, Little Miya. It would be too sad to part ways with you."

"Yes. I'm morbid. I'm unseemly. Because I'm going to kill you."

"Fine. Go ahead."

The boy's lips on her breast reminded her of the silver tea bowl.

Since Keita's father had given it to her, she had tried several times to fill the bowl with her breast, but it no longer fit.

Behind the Ear

I

When Momoko awoke, the Takemiya boy had vanished.

Even after opening her eyes, she felt as though she were still dreaming.

"Oh. He's gone," she tried murmuring, but she was unable to find her voice, and the words sounded in her mind alone.

Her head felt numb.

She tried falling asleep once more to that pleasant numbness. All of a sudden, she remembered that she had already awoken once during the long autumn night.

"Maybe Little Miya killed me?"

With that thought, she snapped wide awake.

She lifted her hand to her neck. The gold necklace too was gone.

"He must have taken it."

A wave of calm washed over her.

She hadn't checked to see whether the boy was lying beside her when she had opened her eyes in the middle of the night.

She remembered hearing birds chirping. At the time, she had thought that it had still been night, but perhaps it had actually been around dawn? It had felt even more like a waking dream than the present moment, as though she had been revived from a deathlike state, only to fall once more into suspended animation.

In fact, she had indeed fallen asleep last night feigning death.

Before that, the boy had pulled at her neck from behind as he called out her name. "Momoko. Momoko."

"It hurts. You're hurting me."

"You won't even look at me. I can't stand it."

"What's the matter? There's no need for me to turn around."

"You make me so miserable."

"Miserable? Is that so, Little Miya?"

"I'm serious. I'm in agony here, always watching you from behind."

"I like looking at the back of your neck."

"You have strange tastes." The boy gently wrapped his arms around her neck. "Why do you enjoy hugging me like this so much?"

Momoko often embraced him from behind, and she had instructed him to hold her that way as well.

It had been the same with the Nishida boy before him, and with the others too.

That day, when Asako had seen her wearing her hair up, she had felt suddenly embarrassed. After all, her real reason for tying it back had been so that the boy could kiss her neck.

Having Takemiya point this out to her now only threw her into a state of confusion.

"It's more heartwarming not to look at each other."

"Heartwarming? That isn't true. My heart feels warmer when I see my reflection in your eyes. You've got a guilty conscience, haven't you?"

"I've done you wrong, Little Miya. It's true."

"You're playing me for a fool. You don't love me."

"This again? You shouldn't say that so easily. You're so quick to say I don't love you, to say I'm going to abandon you. If you keep it up, you'll spend the rest of your life pushing people away."

"You're still treating me like a fool. Every time you turn your back to me, you're thinking about something else."

Momoko shook her head against her pillow. The Takemiya boy pulled at her necklace so hard that it pressed up against her chin.

But hearing these accusations, she found her emotions cooling.

After a short silence, she said, "Look behind my ear, Little Miya. Between my ears and my hairline, the line that stretches to the nape of my neck. I can't hide my age there."

"I can see it," the boy answered offhandedly. "It's so nice, so beautiful. When I look behind your ears, I feel like I'm looking into your soul. It's so tender, so clear and pure."

"You're a good liar. If you really mean that, you aren't looking deeply at all. You're only seeing me from behind."

As Momoko spoke, the boy pressed his lips behind her ears.

She drew her shoulders back sharply.

"You know, I noticed it, back when we were in the bath. The line of your shoulders, from your neck to the base of your arms. It makes such a beautiful arc. I can't even describe it. It's a perfect curve."

The boy wrapped his fingers around her upper arm, squeezing it softly.

"You really are a good liar," Momoko murmured.

The boy increased the strength of his grip before relaxing his hand and sliding his palm across to her breast.

"When you turn your back on me, I feel like I'm always chasing after you. It puts me so on edge."

Momoko was again struck with revulsion at Takemiya's girlish behavior.

It had been precisely those feminine qualities of his that had driven her to seduce him, that had made him such an easy target.

Nonetheless, it hadn't taken long for her to begin to find his mannerisms cloying.

At first, she had attributed that side of him to a spoiled upbringing at the hands of a good family. Perhaps, she wondered, his precociousness was all just an act?

She had felt a masculine sense of superiority over him and had made him into an older woman's plaything. It might be fun, she thought, to toy with him, to treat him with a small helping of cruelty.

Loving the Takemiya boy, she found herself imagining that the person in her arms was really a younger girl.

However, she soon realized that his effeminacy was evidence of his own homosexual leanings.

And with that realization, she recognized too that the Nishida boy had had a similar predisposition.

She hadn't been able to love the Takemiya boy as a woman was supposed to love a man. Perhaps she was disconsolate that their relationship had been soiled by the same-sex attraction that they each harbored?

"I'm pathological," she berated herself. "Sordid."

But she would sometimes throw those same words at the boy too.

Nonetheless, she felt as though it was she who would be left behind, as though it was she who would be rendered disconsolate.

The boy had followed her around everywhere, like a girl. But perhaps he had seen in her only a means of knowing woman, of escaping his latent homosexuality?

The boy's skin may have been as smooth as a girl's, but his bones and flesh were unmistakably different. With time, his masculinity would become only more pronounced.

Momoko's body too had changed.

The silver tea bowl that Keita had made no longer fit. When she had tried placing her breast inside it, she had startled to find how much it had grown.

But had she really become a woman?

Her sense of fear, her resistance toward the kind of relationship that normally existed between men and women, had yet to be wiped away.

She had simply let those youths pass through her cold body.

Takemiya, being particularly sensitive, had realized that something was amiss. He had noticed that something was eating away at her, filling her with sadness.

But her pride wouldn't allow her to reveal the secrets of her feminine body.

Would she have to break up with him before he grew into a man?

Now that they had come to Hakone, she intended to end their relationship.

"What are you thinking, Momoko?" Takemiya whispered in her ear.

"You're an annoying one, aren't you?"

"You didn't talk to me on the bus on the way here either."

"There was nothing to say."

"You could have at least looked at me."

"I did."

"That's a lie."

"It's getting harder for me to look at you, Little Miya."

"Because you're planning to abandon me, aren't you?"

True though that may have been, Momoko's thoughts were directed not to this boy but to Natsuji, who had called at her house that day.

Why had she fled to avoid meeting him? Why had she felt as though she couldn't stand to be in the same building as him?

Even after leaving the house and journeying first by bus, then by boat, still she had been ill at ease, unable to calm her racing thoughts.

Both Natsuji and his father resembled Keita so much. It would be too great a stress on her aching heart to meet him, she had thought.

Nor was she kind enough to keep quietly out of the way if her sister truly did love him.

She didn't understand herself.

However, there was no doubt that the sense of emptiness that had driven her all the way to Hakone with the Takemiya boy had taken root when Natsuji had called.

"Little Miya," she called out. "Little Miya. Have you ever fought against your own sorrow?"

"Sorrow?"

"Doesn't it fill you with grief, coming all this way with me?"

The boy writhed. "You're the one plunging me into grief. You're going to abandon me. I'm sure of it."

"If you're so sure, perhaps we *should* part ways," Momoko said before coming out with a lie. "Little Miya. Your mother sent me a letter. She asked me to let you go, to put everything back to the way it was before. So that you could go back to being a good, diligent student again."

"What?" The boy recoiled. "So now you'll lie about my family too?"

"I completely forgot you have a mother and father, Little Miya. I'm sorry."

"No. Don't throw me aside with a lie. That isn't you. At least be honest and say you don't love me. You've never loved anyone."

"I do love someone."

"Yourself, you mean."

"No. Someone who died." Momoko's thoughts turned to Keita, but instead she found herself murmuring, "My mother."

"Your mother? Didn't you say you love your father when we went out on Lake Ashi during the snow?"

"Did I? It's all the same. My mother killed herself out of love for my father."

The boy pressed his face up against the nape of her neck.

Tears began to flow behind her ears, tears that seemed to seep deep into her head.

"I wish I could say I killed you out of love. I really do." The boy's voice was trembling.

"Do it," Momoko whispered. "It's okay."

"If you abandon me, I'll become a rogue. I'll abandon countless women. But I'll do it even better than you."

Momoko startled. "Is that so? You *are* a good liar, Little Miya."

"No, no. Don't do this. Help me, Momoko. You don't know me." All of a sudden, the boy shook her violently. "I won't let you abandon me. I won't let you turn into a demon like this and cast me aside."

The boy wrapped his arm around his neck, pulled her toward him, and shook her once more. "Are you still going to do it? Are you still going to abandon me?"

Momoko's head spun.

The boy's delirious protests rang in her ears.

She was lying facedown, struggling to breathe with his hands wrapped around her throat. Her body was spasming in pain; yet the idea of vanishing into thin air came to her almost as a relief.

All of a sudden, the boy released his grip.

Momoko breathed in a lungful of air. She felt numb.

When she felt his fingers groping for her in the dark, she held her breath, pretending to be dead. Her mind was so blank that she herself couldn't understand what had prompted her to act that way.

She sank into sleep.

When she awoke in the morning, she tried to make her way to the bathroom, but her legs would hardly support her.

As she washed her neck, she understood with some satisfaction that the boy had taken her gold necklace.

She couldn't say precisely why, but she hadn't had the faintest doubt that he might kill her. Even she herself wondered at the ease with which she had been able to descend into a numbed state of sleep, without offering any resistance, without fearing that she might never wake up.

2

After returning from her trip to Hakone with the Takemiya boy, Momoko became reluctant to leave the house, holing herself up indoors.

She would sit for long hours in front of the sewing machine, taking charge of adjusting Asako's summer clothes.

She set to repurposing her sister's old garments, sewing them anew into more modern designs.

"You don't need to worry about all this," said Asako, who shared her passion for dressmaking. "I feel bad, making you do all this work."

"I want to, so let me be. You don't have to wear them. Then again, knowing you, you'll probably feel obligated to wear them even if you don't like them." There was no irony in Momoko's voice.

"But if I let you do it all, there won't be anything left for me to do. That will make me feel even more uncomfortable."

"I suppose it will. Asako . . ."

"It's like there's nothing left for me to do but the laundry."

"Go do that, then."

"Yes."

Momoko let out a chuckle before glancing across to her sister. "You're a bothersome one, aren't you? You don't have to worry so much."

"Oh?"

"I've noticed, you know? How even with Father, you're always so attentive, always on tenterhooks. I thought maybe my jealousy was clouding my judgment, but no. No, you wound him with your actions. But I'm guessing you haven't even realized that, have you?"

"No, I haven't."

"I thought as much. Maybe that was a bit of an exaggeration. But you do look so much like your mother. I wonder whether she didn't have the same attitude toward him too?"

Momoko's voice was soft, but her words stung Asako's heart.

Her observation seemed to Asako like the kind of cold, distant comment that only a stepchild could come out with.

"Don't you think you're weaving a fine net of concern around Father? It's like a beautiful spiderweb, shining with a silver gleam in the spring sun as the wind blows lightly around it. That's how it looks to me."

"I don't really know." Asako could offer only the vaguest of responses.

But she asked herself whether she and her sister might not have been fighting for their father's affections.

Lately, she had found herself hesitating whenever she thought to speak to either of them.

For her part, Momoko thought back to the pair of sisters whom she had spotted at the inn at Gōra in Hakone.

When it was time to leave, she had wanted to ask the maid

whether the Takemiya boy had returned to Tōkyō, or else was just prowling around somewhere meaning to return, but she hadn't been able to bring herself to broach the subject.

She stared out at the garden as she swallowed down her breakfast, trying not to meet the maid's gaze. The food stuck in her throat.

The inn had originally been a villa owned by the Fujishima conglomerate, and even though there were only seven or eight guest rooms, the garden was maybe four or five acres in size.

The garden resembled a natural forest, sloping toward the valley. The trees were planted closely together, rendering the gardeners' handiwork inconspicuous.

In front of Momoko's room was a large chestnut tree.

A woman's voice echoed across the garden. Glancing around, Momoko spotted a young lady calling out to her sister.

"They're sisters," the maid said to her. "They look so alike."

"Almost identical. How mysterious."

"Yes, indeed. And their little ones are almost the exact same age too."

"Are they here with their husbands?"

"Yes. And the ladies' mother too."

"Do they take after their mother in looks?"

The sisters passed in front of Momoko's room as they made their way down the garden path.

There was no gentleness to the curve of their wide eyes, but their fair-skinned cheeks were beautiful, their features well-defined, and their hair thick from roots to tip.

The older of the two was probably around four years Momoko's junior.

They were each carrying an infant on their backs. The two children didn't look to have yet turned one.

The two mothers were wearing *yukatas* provided by the hotel, while their children were dressed in identical red kimonos—gifts from their grandmother, Momoko supposed.

The two sisters were surrounded by fresh, verdant foliage. Azaleas lined both sides of the path weaving through the garden, and while they were no longer in bloom, the leaves hid the sisters from view from the chest down.

From a short distance away, they looked just like twins.

The image of the sisters carrying their children on their backs, clothed in red among the greenery, had, for Momoko, the feel of a sacred painting.

But when they turned their backs to her, she realized that their necks were somewhat stocky and fat, vulgar even, calling to mind a pair of wild boars. That impression was only accentuated by the presence of the children on their backs.

"Hmm." Momoko laughed at herself.

The way in which the two sisters resembled one another, and the sight of their young children, had awoken in her a sense of hallowed joy; but that feeling may have been overshadowed by the weakness in her heart now that the Takemiya boy was gone.

She later pondered whether it might not have been divine providence, or perhaps human triumph, that she and Asako looked so unalike.

Afterward, the Takemiya boy called her on the telephone several times.

Not once, however, had Momoko answered.

He even came to visit her at home. He had refused to leave despite the maid's protestations.

"Shall I talk to him?" Asako suggested.

"Yes. Perhaps your meddling could come in handy. Tell him I'm dead, please."

"What?"

"He'll understand."

Around an hour later, Asako returned upstairs, a worried look on her face. "Momoko! I thought he was alone, but there was another boy with him, someone called Nishida."

"Oh? How childish of him."

"And there were two more as well. Four in all."

"Oh?"

"They said they felt the same way, that they were all sorry for Miya and had decided to end their lives together. They insisted on seeing you."

"You should have just told them nothing could possibly make me happier."

"Momoko, you shouldn't go outside. It's dangerous."

"Oh, they're all so meek." Momoko frowned. "Give it a decade. By then, I'll be the only one still burdened by these wounds."

Asako watched her sister in silence.

"They say time heals all ills. But that seems to apply only to men. There's a line in *The Letters of a Portuguese Nun*: *It is only since I have been employing all my efforts to heal myself that I have come to know the excesses of my love.* You should take care yourself, Asako."

Asako approached the window and looked out onto the street.

The boys were gone.

"How tanned you are!" Momoko observed.

"I've been playing tennis."

"Your skin really has turned dark."

"But I like summer."

"Do you always go to the tennis club with Natsuji?"

"No."

Momoko sat down in front of the sewing machine before her sister could leave the window.

Ten days later, Asako was hospitalized with acute pleurisy. Natsuji came to call on her at the house.

Momoko realized that Asako mustn't have told him about her illness. She was strangely moved by her sister's touchingly pitiful nature.

"I have to go to the museum for my father. It won't take long, so why don't you join me? My sister is out, by the way," she said.

Natsuji nodded. "Ah. I'll be going back to Kyōto for the summer break, so I thought I'd call before I go. I have a message for you too, from my dad. He'd like you to come visit us in Kyōto. He asked me to accompany you when I go back."

"Oh? Thank you."

When she left the museum, Momoko found Natsuji lying on the lawn beneath the leaves of the cherry trees.

As they strolled through Ueno Park toward Hirokōji Street, Momoko asked, "You were born in summer, weren't you, Natsuji?"

"Yes, just like my name. *Natsu* for summer, *ji* because I'm the second son. I was born in August. That said, I can't handle the heat very well."

"It gets hot in Kyōto, doesn't it?"

"Yes. I do love summer, though."

Momoko suppressed a smile before asking with an air of indifference, "Is that why you're so tanned? Have you been playing tennis?"

"That's right. See how dark my skin is now?"

Momoko remembered how dark Keita's skin had become during his time in the military.

She caught the smell of summer from Natsuji's masculine body. Keita had smelled that way too.

She slowly increased the distance between herself and Natsuji as they walked.

Having grown accustomed to staying at home, she couldn't stand the harsh sunlight.

The Painted Rainbow

I

It was autumn by the time Asako was finally well enough to leave the hospital.

Every day during her convalescence, she had contemplated a painting of a rainbow hanging on the wall of her hospital room.

It was a color reproduction of Millet's *Spring*.

No sooner had she been strong enough to step out into the corridor to use the telephone than she called her father. "I wish I at least had some pictures to look at. Next time you come visit, could you bring that collection of Fujishima Takeji's works?"

"The big volume? I suppose so, but it's quite heavy. You probably won't be able to leaf through it lying down."

"Yes. But there's a picture of a rainbow in it."

"A picture of a rainbow? A rainbow, you said?"

"Yes. A picture of a rainbow over a lake."

"I see. But we also have a reproduction of a painting by Millet. There's a rainbow in that one too. You probably don't remember it, do you?"

"A painting by Millet? I don't recall."

"I didn't think so. I wonder where I put it. I'll try to fish it out, and I'll bring it along with the Fujishima collection," her father said over the telephone.

Reading through the book, Asako discovered that the painting by Fujishima Takeji was titled *Quiet* and had been featured in an exhibition run by the Ministry of Education in 1916. Of course, that was before she had been born.

On the other hand, Millet's *Spring*, or *Rainbow*, as it was also known, had been exhibited at the Paris Salon almost eighty years earlier, in 1868, before even her father had entered the world.

The previous year, Millet had presented nine separate works at the Exposition Universelle, where he won first prize and was awarded a medal by the government. There, at the age of fifty-five, after countless long and grueling battles, he finally achieved a period of recognition and success.

However, it seemed that *Spring* had been exhibited unfinished. The artist didn't complete the work until six years later, in 1874, one year before his death. For that reason, it was widely regarded as his final masterpiece.

"Have you really forgotten it, Asako?" her father asked when he came to visit her.

"I don't remember . . ."

"Oh." Her father seemed unconvinced. "Well, you were still so small. I suppose I didn't hang it up again after you got bigger."

"I haven't seen it before."

"I see, I see. I bought reproductions of a few famous paint-ings during my trip to the West. The others I gave away, but your mother liked this one, so we kept it."

"She liked it?"

"She did. So much so that she framed it and hung it up in her room."

Asako sat up in her bed. "I like it too."

She stared at the reproduction as she wiped the glass with her sleeve. "There's a rainbow here in the corner."

"Indeed."

"And are these apple blossoms?"

The picture showed three or four apple trees decorated with white flowers among the tender herbs of a field in early spring. The woods on the other side of the hill were a similar youthful green. The earth was a moist red in color, and a rain-bow hung overhead against black rain clouds.

The rainbow was in the upper-left corner of the image, its arc extending outside the frame. Was it supposed to signify the blessings of spring growth?

When Momoko came to call on her, Asako had already hung the painting on the wall of her hospital room.

Nonetheless, her sister sat with her back to the wall and so didn't notice it.

"Father brought me that picture there, Momoko," Asako said.

Her sister glanced over her shoulder. "Oh?"

She rose to her feet and stepped back to get a better look at it, resting her hand on the headboard of the bed. "Well, now. So this painting has made its way here too, has it?"

"Do you remember it, Momoko?"

"I do."

"Oh? I don't. Father thought I might, but I simply couldn't picture it."

"That doesn't surprise me."

"He said Mother liked it."

"Yes, I suppose she did. She hung it in her room."

"Really? You remember that too?"

"Of course I do. I couldn't possibly forget. It was hanging in her room the same day Father brought me in from the countryside."

Asako startled.

"It left a strong impression on me," Momoko continued. "When you fell sick, you must have reminded Father of her. No doubt that's why he brought it here. So Mother's spirit would watch over you."

"That isn't it at all. I asked him to bring me the book of Fujishima Takeji's paintings, and he said we had a reproduction of a picture of a rainbow by Millet too." Asako held out the volume. "I remembered the rainbow I saw over Lake Biwa, so I wanted to take a look at this one here. See? It's called *Quiet*."

"Oh?"

"Father brought the Millet painting back as a souvenir from the West."

"Oh? I'm another of his *souvenirs from the West*, you know?" Momoko hesitated for a moment before continuing, her voice flat, as though it was a matter of no real consequence, "He must have remembered my mother and me during his faraway travels. That was when he confided in your mother, by letter. Your mother married him even knowing he already had a child by another woman. But my mother died without him ever marrying her, and I was left in her house in the countryside. He should have forgotten about me, treated it as all over and done with. But maybe his overseas travels threw a pall over your mother's spirits."

At times like this, Momoko would refer pointedly to *your mother* and *my mother*.

Those terms never failed to grate on Asako's ears.

That her father, during an overseas trip while she had been but a mere baby, had sorrowfully remembered a woman other than her mother, and a child whom he had had with her at that, was a reality that she found difficult to accept, even if it no longer caused her undue distress.

"So the fact that you have an elder sister is practically another of his *souvenirs from the West*," Momoko said before adding, "I saw this painting the very day he brought me to my new home."

Asako glanced again at the picture on the wall. "I don't remember."

"Your mother was holding you on her lap the day I first met you. You were staring at me so strangely. Your mother kept saying you must have been so happy now that your elder sister had arrived, but even then, you seemed so bashful. You kept glancing back toward her and reaching for her breast. Maybe you were hungry. It made me feel sad. And jealous too. Back in the countryside, everyone told me I was going to meet my new mother. And there she was, looking so much like my own mother, holding a child on her lap. But I remember thinking she wasn't *my* mother."

"I don't remember," Asako murmured.

"Of course you don't. How old were you when you learned we were born to different mothers?"

"Around six or seven."

"Yes, around seven. It was excruciating for me up to then. The legitimate daughter ignorant of the truth known by the illegitimate one. If I had been the legitimate daughter, I would have protected you from it. But I wasn't, and so I've always had to live with the fact that I robbed you of something. You cried when you learned the truth. And I started trembling all over. When you saw me shaking, you were so surprised that you stopped crying."

"Yes, I remember that."

"Later, I wondered why I had ended up trembling so much. I was a terribly stubborn child. Even I knew that, and I hated myself for it. I even managed to convince myself that you must have had some inkling of the truth all along."

Asako shook her head.

"No, I couldn't help it, that trembling. And I forbade you to tell Father or Mother what you had learned, didn't I?"

"It was so long ago." Asako lay down on her side and pulled her blanket up to her shoulders.

"Yes, we should drop the subject. That painting brought back a lot of memories, that's all."

Momoko turned her back to it, returning to her chair against the wall.

"Hiroshige has a famous woodblock print of a rainbow too, you know? Where did I see it? Probably in an art book somewhere. A slender rainbow stretching over the sea. The scene was of the old Susaki district, I think."

"There are a lot of pictures of rainbows, aren't there?"

"Indeed. Hiroshige's is called *Haze on a Clear Day at*

Susaki and is part of his *Eight Views of Edo* series. Who's to say it doesn't have any connection with Lake Biwa? Shall I bring the art book with Hiroshige's works next time?"

"Please."

"Yes, that picture of the rainbow at Susaki has such a soft, ephemeral feeling."

Momoko, perhaps trying to change the subject, began talking about Hiroshige's woodblock prints.

But all this talk about Momoko's childhood had prompted Asako too to reflect on her past.

The memories of these two half sisters belonged to different currents, refusing to flow together.

Momoko stared up at the painting on the wall once more. "There's an intense strength, a profound sense of joy in the Millet painting here, isn't there? When I saw this picture after coming in from the countryside, I felt like I was about to embark on an elegant, dazzling new life. When I learned I was going to live in Father's house from then on, to my childish mind, it was like I had discovered a rainbow inside my own heart."

Was she trying to say that that rainbow had since disappeared?

When Momoko had first laid eyes on that painting, Asako had been sitting on her mother's lap; and yet she couldn't remember any of it.

And of course, Momoko remembered Asako's mother from that time better than she herself did.

To Asako, this realization struck her as unreasonable, uncanny.

Deep in her heart, might she not harbor a sense of jealousy, of hostility even, directed toward her elder sister?

Young children could be selfish at times, and unexpectedly mean-spirited. What had she, as a young girl, thought from the safety of her mother's lap as she stared across at this new half sister just arrived from the countryside? Might she not have greeted her with all the scorn and hatred of which a three-year-old child was capable?

She couldn't remember, and so the thought only gnawed at her all the more.

"You wanted to see this painting; yes, because you're unwell, but also because your mother adored it so much while you were just a baby, perhaps?" Momoko asked.

That accusation struck a chord in Asako's heart. "No. I remembered the rainbow I saw over Lake Biwa last winter. That was why."

"A winter rainbow? That image doesn't suit you. But it might suit me. You're better off thinking about spring rainbows, like in Millet's picture here."

"But I'm not like you think."

"You're right, of course. Maybe I corrupted your personality when I trespassed into your family while you were just a baby? You've been different ever since I told you we were born to different mothers. You started treating me with extra kindness. Even now, you're excessively considerate of others. That must be why. I told you the truth too soon."

"But I would have found out sooner or later, once I started counting backward from when Mother and Father got married."

"That's true." Momoko nodded, grabbing her left wrist in her right hand and hanging her head. "But you know, even as a child, seeing that kindness of yours, I swore to myself never

to betray you. But I failed. When I'm dead, reduced to nothing more than a pile of bones and ash, then I'll apologize for
what I've done."

"Momoko!" Asako's lightly sunken eyelids quivered.

Her sister may very well have concluded that her illness
had been born of her compassionate nature.

When Natsuji had invited her to play tennis, she threw
herself headfirst into the strenuous sport. She enjoyed playing; but might it not have looked to others as though she had
fervently dedicated herself to it, to such an extent that she
had forgotten herself, because it was what he enjoyed?

Might not even her reluctance to divulge her condition to
him be a twisted consequence of the excessive consideration
that she had for others?

Momoko found her sister endearingly pitiful.

However, even when she met Natsuji, she didn't inform
him of Asako's illness. She couldn't ask him to try to understand her sister's heart.

He may have come to their home asking after her, and
Momoko may have accompanied him to the museum and
around town, but she never told him that her sister had been
admitted to the hospital.

She had even felt a vague titillation that Natsuji hadn't
dared ask her about Asako. There was undeniably a malicious
streak within her, a quality that filled her with a sense of self-
satisfied relish.

Nor, when she herself visited Asako in her hospital room,
did she tell her sister that she had met Natsuji. And she certainly didn't tell her that he had invited her to visit his home
in Kyōto.

In her sister's absence, Momoko had been kept busy in the house, looking after their father and supervising the work in the kitchen.

"Father seems so lonely with you gone. I can't stand it. He always lets you handle everything. I don't know what to do." Momoko shook her head. "I can't even prepare a bowl of broth that tastes the same as yours. No, I can't stand it. I couldn't possibly live alone with him. I would lose my mind."

So she said, yet her soul was aflame with a mysterious passion.

While her stepmother had been alive, Momoko had always held herself at a distance, furtively resisting any attempt to establish a close or affectionate bond with her father.

That habit of hers persisted even now.

She found herself wondering whether her father hadn't deliberately tried to conceal that he had taken the painting, so adored by her stepmother, to Asako's hospital room, and she hated herself for it.

If her sister hadn't been looking, she would have ground her teeth in frustration.

2

The city had been bracing for an approaching typhoon for the past few days, and while the storm changed course at the last minute without making landfall, the hospital had none-theless been buffeted by strong winds since dawn.

Asako had wondered whether she could hear rain drumming against the windowpanes, but it was only the leaves of the ginkgo tree in the garden.

The leaves had just begun to turn yellow. It wasn't yet time for them to fall, but they nonetheless seemed frail and precarious in the face of the storm.

The ginkgo tree was a little taller than the roof of the two-story hospital building.

Over the course of that morning, the leaves were scattered to the wind, revealing the bare branches underneath.

That same morning, Asako had received an unexpected visit from the Takemiya boy.

"Oh! What brings you here?"

"Can I come in?" The boy lingered in the doorway.

"Close the door. It's windy outside," she answered.

The boy did as instructed but approached no closer.

His face seemed even paler than the vivid whiteness of the door.

"Is something the matter? How did you know I was here?" Asako had a vague presentiment.

"Your maid told me."

"Oh?"

"I hid by the wall outside your house and waited for her to come out on an errand. I probably gave her a good scare when she did."

"Oh?"

By now, Asako was well enough to move around. She carefully arranged her collar and the hem of her arrow feather–patterned silk kimono and sat down on the edge of her bed.

"She said your sister was in Kyōto. And she told me you were here."

"Momoko went to Kyōto?" Asako found herself murmuring aloud, but quickly swallowed her voice.

The maid must have been trying to mislead him.

Then again, the tearoom that her father had designed for Natsuji was apparently almost completed, and she had heard that they had been invited to try it for themselves.

Her father had half-heartedly suggested that they might go to Kyōto when she was feeling better; but perhaps Momoko had decided to go on ahead?

But even so, what could have brought Takemiya to call on her in the middle of a storm?

That question weighed so heavily on her mind that she found herself knotting her obi almost without thinking.

"I'm going to go to Kyōto too," the boy said.

Maybe it was because he had just been out in the wind, but the boy's face was pink all the way to his ears, as though he had just braved a winter chill.

Yet when he had entered the room, only his lips appeared red.

Asako's heart began to beat more slowly. "To see my sister?"

"Yes."

"What will you do when you find her?"

"I don't know. At worst, I might kill her, or maybe myself. I won't trouble anyone else."

Asako felt as though she had just brushed up against the cold skin of a lizard.

"Did you come here to tell me that?"

"No. I wanted to let you know I'm grateful to you." The boy's voice took on a hollow tone. "You were so nice when I called at your home that time. After talking with you, I felt more relaxed when I left."

"Oh? But there were four of you. I thought you were all so cowardly. I lost my temper. It was like you were all having a bit of fun."

"I see." The boy averted his gaze. "I also wanted to return your sister's necklace. Could you give it back to her for me?"

The boy pulled a gold necklace from his pocket, approached her bed, and placed it on the edge of her blanket.

"Why do you have that?"

"I stole it. I'd be a coward to keep it. I've burned everything else she gave me. I'm going to settle things with her."

"Settle things? There's no need to go that far. Can't you hold off on chasing after her? Won't you wait awhile? Ten years, maybe? If you still feel the same about her after all that, you can do it then."

"I don't have that long to live."

Asako felt a sudden chill. "Five years. Three, even."

"What do you think of your sister, Asako?"

She was unable to quickly formulate a response to this sudden question.

"I came here to return the necklace, so I'll be going now. I wanted to see you too. I'm sorry to disturb you while you're ill. That's all. Take care."

The boy spun around. As he left, Asako noticed that he had let his hair grow out, covering the nape of his neck.

Nonetheless, it was the almost greenish pallor of his countenance that remained etched in her mind.

She lay down on her side, squeezed her eyes shut, and covered her face in her hands.

Her palms felt a little cold.

When the wind died down, she opened her eyes to a swirling mass of thick dark clouds.

She telephoned her father.

He was apparently planning to visit Kyōto in four or five days' time.

"Is Momoko going with you?"

"Yes, she's coming too. You could come with us as well, Asako, seeing as your doctor says you can come home now. But why don't we take it easy? You'll probably be better off staying where you are a little longer than coming back to an empty house."

"Is Momoko at home now?"

"She went out when the wind eased up. What a terrible storm! How is everything at the hospital?"

In the end, Asako missed her chance to tell her father that the Takemiya boy had called on her, and that he would be making his way to Kyōto too.

3

Momoko and her father took the Hato limited express service on the Tōkaidō Main Line.

The second-class seats in the new passenger carriage could be reclined up to forty-five degrees and had footrests that could be raised and lowered to three different heights. There were also electronic loudspeakers so that the conductor could address the passengers.

Mizuhara immediately tilted his seat back as far as it would go and stretched out his body.

Momoko considered following suit, before stopping herself. After all, she remembered, she seemed to be pregnant with the Takemiya boy's child.

Her pregnancy didn't show yet, but she was nonetheless reluctant to risk drawing attention to herself.

She had had her suspicions even before leaving for Kyōto.

She found herself contemplating the shifting scenery outside the window.

Red flowers dotted a chrysanthemum field beside a farmhouse, and beyond that, white-feathered chickens could be seen flocking inside their wire pens.

A grove of persimmons was beginning to ripen in color.

The beautifully tiled roofs of the houses lining the old Mikawa Road were still dark and glistening from rain the previous night.

Autumn-colored waves crested over the sandy beaches of Lake Hamana.

At around that point, the train came to an unexpected stop.

"We apologize for the delay. We're presently waiting for the signal to change," came a voice over the loudspeaker.

When the train finally resumed its journey, Momoko rose to her feet.

The men's bathroom was situated at the front of the carriage, while the women's was located at the back.

The pressing urge that she had been holding in was, she suspected, another symptom of her pregnancy.

Autumn Leaves

I

Accompanying her father, Momoko visited the Ginkakuji Temple and the Hōnen'in Temple before returning to their inn at Sanjō.

"I forget who it was who said that walking the streets of Kyōto is like traveling along a highland plateau, but the weather today really does give you that impression, doesn't it?" So her father had said during their outing, coming to a stop to stare up at the clear autumn sky.

After leaving the Ginkakuji, the two of them made their way up a winding mountain road until they reached the black gate leading into the Hōnen'in.

It was too late in the season for them to view the second blooming of the irises in the pond, and too early to see the camellia flowers for which the temple was renowned, but the maples were awash with red foliage, and the running water echoed across the garden with its white sand sculptures.

The temple grounds were filled to abundance with camellia trees, to which the abbot was said to have dedicated many a haiku verse.

Not far from the Hōnen'in was the Anrakuji Temple at Mount Jūren, and the graves of Suzumushi and Matsumushi, former ladies of the court of the emperor Go-Toba. Momoko had heard the story before.

The emperor Go-Toba was said to have been furious when his two favorite mistresses, charmed by the monks Anraku and Jūren, abandoned the court to join the Buddhist reformer Hōnen's fledgling Pure Land sect. As a result, Go-Toba condemned Anraku and Jūren to death and exiled their leader Hōnen to Tosa Province on the island of Shikoku.

Now, however, the temple lay deserted, overgrown with weeds.

South of the Anrakuji stood the Reikanji Temple in Shishigatani.

From there, Momoko and her father followed the canal first to the Nyakuōji Temple, then to the Nanzenji Temple.

The Aoki residence wasn't far from the Nanzenji.

"I think the cherry trees along the canal at the Nyakuōji are the most beautiful in all of Kyōto," Aoki had said back in spring.

Momoko and Asako had caught their breath at the sight of a large maple at the Nyakuōji, which they had admired for some time. The deep blue color of the sky, peeking through gaps in the rich foliage, had struck them as a truly Japanese autumnal pattern.

Momoko had hoped to catch another glimpse of that maple, but her heart grew heavy at the thought of the child she was carrying in her womb. She parted ways with her father, who went on to visit Aoki, and returned to the inn.

There, she encountered a maid whom she hadn't seen during her stay in the spring.

The maid identified herself as the daughter of a former navy captain. "Although he considers himself forever a *mere* navy captain."

"He was a captain? But that's a rather lofty position! What did he do, exactly?"

"He was in command of a submarine. He keeps saying that old navy men like him aren't good for anything now with the war over, that he wants to be called back into service so he can die at sea."

"I see. There might well be another war if they blockade the coasts of Korea and China. But here in Japan, weren't all our submarines sunk?"

"Who knows? I don't have time to listen to those stories anymore."

The captain's daughter went on to explain that her husband had died during the war, lost with his ship.

Now, she was left alone with her two children, the eldest of whom was in her second year of elementary school.

Momoko stared at the maid in astonishment. "Imagine that! You're so pretty, and you look so young. Yes, so young. I thought you must be younger than I am."

"What are you saying, miss? You're the pretty one."

Despite her slightly puffy eyelids, the maid, with her oval face, embodied the typical Kyōto ideal of beauty.

The woman, an only daughter whose mother had passed away and whose late husband had been adopted into her family, explained that she was unable to entrust her children to her own father, the former navy captain, and so had taken on this work in a somewhat irregular manner, commuting daily to the inn rather than living on-site.

"It's difficult when you don't live on the premises. You have to really think what to do about your clothes. The kimonos are expensive, and you have to buy them even if you don't want to. And then you earn less than the live-in maids. I normally take the last train home, and I only really get to see my children's faces in the mornings. I'm constantly busy preparing everyone's lunches, and then enough sides for dinner later. My eldest is a girl, and she's noticed that our bowls grow emptier by the week. All I can do is ask her to bear with it, tell her this is all because her grandfather lost the war."

"It can't be easy, a young woman alone providing for a family of four on a maid's salary," Momoko remarked.

"I often think that if I only had the one child, if it were only the two of us, I might be able to manage. But I can't work any harder than I already do."

"Oh?" Momoko began before falling silent.

She found herself wondering what her own life would have been like if she had had a child with Keita, who, like the woman's husband, had similarly died in the war.

Perhaps next year, she would have to work too, to support not Keita's child but the Takemiya boy's?

The maid went on to explain that she had started working in June, but no sooner had she begun than she had been forced to take time off after coming down with a lung condition during the rainy season. She had returned to work only recently, to earn enough money to buy clothes for her children for the winter.

"I still feel a heavy feeling here when I push myself too hard," she said, placing a hand against her shoulder.

"My sister was hospitalized recently for her lungs too. We stayed here together in the spring, but she was admitted to the hospital not too long ago. It was playing tennis that caused her illness, though."

"Well, we're of different social stations."

But Asako too had a passionate temperament. In Momoko's view, she had fallen ill because she had devoted herself to the sport with too much ardor to please Natsuji.

"Social stations? What an old-fashioned expression!" Momoko laughed.

Nonetheless, the real target of her mirth, she knew, was herself.

What would this strange new world bring her tomorrow, after stripping yesterday's submarine commander of his pension and leaving him to live today on the auspices of his daughter?

"I wonder whether anyone in today's Japan can really claim to have a firm social status? It might only be people like you, carrying the weight of three other family members all by yourself, who truly know where they stand," Momoko said.

"Maybe so, but there's nothing certain about my line of work, or about my health either. All I know for sure is that I have four mouths to feed."

The maid explained that she was thinking of selling the house that she was presently letting out to start a small business, but that the three tenant families already living there would be unlikely to vacate the property.

Such stories were by no means unusual; indeed, they could be found in abundance in the present day and age.

But Momoko found it difficult to identify the banal image of a widow in the woman sitting in front of her, with her beautiful mouth and attractive cheeks.

"Get married," she suggested lightly.

"As if I could! What with all these young girls unable to find a husband, not even a middle-aged man would want someone like me, bringing three extra mouths to feed! And I've seen too much of what men like to get up to since I started working here. I couldn't trust anyone."

"Then find a lover. Even if you work yourself to the bone, you'll get no thanks in this new age."

"All right. I'll let you introduce me to someone, miss."

This former navy captain's daughter, it seemed, could now bring herself to come out with a joke.

Momoko, however, was amazed at herself for being so forward as to advise a war widow to become another man's mistress.

Even more astonishing was that it was Keita's father who had come to mind as the other party.

Aoki lived alone, and so any such relationship would be of harm to no one. Perhaps the maid would be able to properly recuperate from her lung condition that way too?

But it was such a strange reverie.

Why, Momoko wondered, had her sympathy for the maid called to mind Keita's father? Neither the maid nor Aoki seemed to be of impure character. It was she, who had thought of them together like that, whose mind was sullied.

"But you need to take care of what matters most to you. No matter how hard it is, there will come a time when you thank yourself for it," Momoko said gently. "Although it isn't for me to say what's important to you."

"Well, I wonder . . . I must say, no one has ever spoken to me like this before, miss. I was so happy when I was assigned to take care of your room. At first, I thought it was because you're so pretty, but now . . ."

The maid folded Momoko's scarf, put her overcoat away, and brought her a warm hand towel.

Momoko sat absorbed in her thoughts with a cup of warm bancha tea in her hands.

"Momoko," came a voice as the fusuma panel slid open.

Without any prior announcement, the Takemiya boy appeared, standing outside the room. He had let his hair grow long.

"Little Miya?" Momoko called out to him calmly. "Come inside. Sit down."

The boy knelt demurely on the other side of the table. He looked to have lost weight, and his temples were pale in color.

"I'm here, Momoko," was all that he said.

"Oh? Welcome," she answered, a little shy. "You went to see my sister at the hospital, didn't you, Little Miya?"

"Yes."

"Why?"

"To return your necklace."

"I received it. But why not give it back to me in person? My sister has nothing to do with us."

"Yes. But I wanted to say farewell to her too."

"*Farewell?* What's that supposed to mean, *farewell*?"

"I'm saying farewell to this world," the boy replied without hesitation.

"Oh? Do you plan to die, Little Miya?"

"Yes."

"Do you expect to startle me, saying that? You certainly did your best to surprise my sister, didn't you?"

"Not exactly . . ."

"Don't you think it's strange to say goodbye to her before me? With her generous spirit, maybe you thought she would sympathize with just about anyone?"

"I didn't want her sympathy. I only wanted to thank her."

"What would *you* have to thank Asako for, Little Miya?"

"I'd like her to keep on living once I'm gone. So I went to see if she was recovering."

"And?" Momoko's heart was still. "So now you're satisfied she's going to live, you've come to kill me. Is that it, Little Miya?"

"That's right," the boy nodded, his clear eyes shining. "There's nothing left to discuss. Nothing at all, right?"

"Yes. Maybe there is nothing. I'm happy to let you kill me, Little Miya. But you won't. Because I've already thought so much about dying myself."

"You're making fun of me now."

"There's something I've wanted to tell you, Little Miya. You've been with a man, haven't you? I know. So why is it me you want to kill, and not that man of yours?"

Takemiya didn't answer.

"Live as a man. Those are my parting words for you. Love between two men won't bring you any children."

Nonetheless, he seemed not to have heard her.

"If you die here, Little Miya, your life will have been for nothing."

"I don't want you to abandon me."

"Oh? Then why do you want to kill me? You'll want to strangle me, I suppose? But you've already tried so many times."

"I can't do it. I'm not capable of it. I know that," the boy said, rising unsteadily to his feet.

He circled around and wrapped an arm around her neck.

Momoko did nothing to object.

"You're okay, Momoko? Tell me when it hurts. I'll loosen my grip . . ." Takemiya's hand was trembling.

"Such a strange child. Let me see your face a little," she said, wondering whether her child would resemble its father.

The boy leaned over Momoko's right shoulder, his tears spilling onto the table.

Momoko closed her eyes.

But as soon as she noticed that Takemiya's arm was pressing too hard on her throat, she screamed in a hoarse voice, "Stop, Miya! Stop! I'm carrying your child! Your child is inside me!"

As expected, the boy loosened his arm.

Momoko at once felt unexpectedly bashful at her own words and was struck by a sudden tenderness for the boy.

"A child?" Takemiya pressed his face against her back. "You're lying. You're a liar. A child? But *I'm* a child."

"You're not a child, Little Miya."

Momoko felt the warmth of Takemiya's face seep through her back and into her body. Her heart began to beat faster.

"My mother died after giving birth to me. But do you

want to kill me even before that?" She felt herself overflowing with tenderness.

"Tell me you're lying," the boy repeated.

"It isn't a lie. I wouldn't lie about something like that."

The boy pulled his face and hands away from her. "It isn't mine, is it? You're lying. It isn't mine."

"Oh? Little Miya?" Momoko felt as though she had been doused with cold water.

"I'm right, aren't I? It isn't my child, is it? *I'm* still a child."

Momoko's heart felt frozen. She shivered. "You're right. It's *my* child. Not yours."

"No." Takemiya stood up, took a few steps back, and stared down at her. "You're lying. You can't fool me."

Then, covering his face with his hands, he let out a low groan before exiting the room.

Momoko didn't move.

She remembered when Keita had embraced her for the first time, only to push her away, hurling her into the indescribable depths of hatred and sadness.

Had the Takemiya boy fled out of jealousy, or out of cowardice?

"*I'm* still a child."

Only those desperate words remained, ringing coldly in her ears.

2

Mizuhara and Momoko were the only guests at Aoki's new tearoom.

Mizuhara didn't comment on the design, having already paid a quick visit to inspect the building on the way back from visiting the Ginkakuji and the Hōnen'in.

"But speaking as the architect, I can't approve of coming in here dressed in Western clothing." He turned to Momoko. "But I suspect Asako would be wearing Western dress too if she had come."

"Not at all. It's me, the owner, who is the dubious one here." Aoki chuckled. "I heard a story from an antiques dealer the other day about a man who doted on the tea ceremony and couldn't wait to perform it in front of guests. He kept practicing with the help of a reference book. The master suggested all the movements while hiding in the preparation area off by the side of the room. But he was such a large, fat fellow that when he grabbed the lid of the kettle, he slammed it down with such force that he ended up shattering a precious lid rest, a Kiseto or an Oribe, I think."

Mizuhara nodded along to the story. "What prodigious strength! Very unusual."

"Indeed. He was from Tōkyō, but he soon earned himself a name here in Kyōto too."

"To think he managed to crush the lid rest."

"My thoughts exactly. Even if I tried to break one, I wouldn't be strong enough to do it." Aoki drummed his hand a couple of times on the lid rest nearby. "Speaking of Western clothes, I spoke to the head of the Urasenke school of the tea ceremony. He said most men who come to him wear Western clothes these days. Before the war, anyone dressed like that wouldn't have been let through the front gate, let alone into a master's tearoom. It would have been considered unbecoming, a breach of basic etiquette."

"Lately, it seems even those hoodlums in Ginza are trying their hand at the tea ceremony. I saw one of them looking at a Shino tea bowl in an antiques shop, asking how much it cost."

"I suppose we aren't all that different, though. But after losing a son in the war, being burned out of my home, moving all the way to Kyōto, and building this quaint little tearoom here, now it's starting all over again in Korea."

"Even Rikyū himself lived during a time of war. There's a poem by Yoshii Isamu on the subject."

"There were no atomic bombs in Rikyū's day. Maybe I should have asked you to build me a bomb shelter before worrying about a tearoom."

"As an architect, I went to look at the devastation at Hiroshima and Nagasaki. When I walk the streets of Kyōto here, when those same eyes take in all this, I shudder to think what might happen if another atomic bomb were to be dropped."

"I can imagine. All we can do is sit around eating boiled tofu and the like and wait quietly to meet whatever the future has in store for us," Aoki said as he poured the tea. "There's a boiled tofu restaurant associated with the Nanzenji nearby. I often go there to spend the evening sitting by the pond with its withered lotuses, surrounded by scattered maple leaves as I watch the sun set. It's hard to believe I live in the same neighborhood. I'm ashamed to admit it, but I've developed a habit of drinking alone. I've even taken to pouring myself a cup of saké here in this tearoom."

A scroll from the Sutra of Past and Present Karma hung in the alcove. It was eighteen lines long. Mizuhara had asked Aoki to show it to him after hearing that he had acquired it in Kyōto.

"It was your father who ordered it," Aoki said, turning

to Momoko. "This sutra was originally written more than a thousand years ago, during the Tempyō era. It doesn't exactly match the decor or the other objects in here, but it was your father's idea. Of course, being as familiar with the tea ceremony as he is, he must have thought it would make an interesting contrast."

"It's a rare pleasure to see a sutra from the eighth century hanging in a tokonoma alcove I designed."

"I wasn't quite sure whether I should put a Buddhist painting on display today, but then I thought it might make a good memorial to Keita. Especially as you're here joining us, Momoko."

A sharp pain pierced Momoko's heart as she looked upon the small images of the buddhas, like dear little dolls.

"I read Keita's diaries after he died. I realized that even though I was his father, I never understood him. I never realized his true worth. He must have gone to his death consumed with loneliness and regret. Maybe that's just what happens between parents and their children."

"Perhaps. I often feel that way with my daughters," Mizuhara answered, avoiding Momoko's gaze.

"But your daughters are both still alive. We're talking about very different things."

"I suppose so."

"I'm hesitant to ask this in your daughter's presence, but did you approve of our children's relationship while my son was alive?" Aoki, his head bowed, placed the tea bowl in front of Momoko. "Please."

"Thank you." Momoko approached on her knees.

Mizuhara faltered. "I wonder . . . I wasn't entirely oblivious to it, but, well, I wanted Momoko to be free to make her own choices."

"I see. I suppose I should say then that you did approve, in some sense. Thank you."

"Not at all."

"For my part, I knew almost nothing. That was one of the things I never realized about my son . . . It must have seemed as if I only approved of their relationship after his death. That was terribly selfish of me, and disrespectful to you, Momoko. You must think I've forced you to keep reliving the past, all so I can hold a memorial to the dead, to confess my sins as a father. When we met at the Saami last spring, I thanked you, and I apologized. I thought we could treat it all as past, as finished. But you said it wasn't. I haven't been able to forget those words ever since."

"In that case, let's acknowledge that Momoko loved your Keita," Mizuhara declared.

"Thank you. But Keita is dead, and when you and I are gone . . ." Aoki wiped the tea bowl with his thick round hands.

For supper, they returned to the tatami-floored room in the house to enjoy a better view of the maples in the garden.

Dinner was a traditional course meal, provided by one of the most famous caterers of tea ceremony cuisine in Kyōto.

Momoko, her heart astir, was unable to make out the different tastes.

After eating, Mizuhara put on a pair of garden clogs and returned to the tearoom.

"The sasanquas by the fence are in bloom," came his voice from afar.

Aoki looked idly toward Momoko. "Please stay with me here in Kyōto for a while."

"Thank you. I will."

"I hear Natsuji has been stopping by your place from time to time. Thank you for looking out for him."

"Yes. You may need to approve of something else soon."

"I understand." Aoki's gaze shone with unusual vitality for a man his age, before clouding over. "Momoko. Is something troubling you?"

She felt her cheeks turning red. He had seen through her.

"I have some experience when it comes to affairs of the heart. Whatever it is, you can talk to me. There's very little that surprises me anymore. I know this may sound like I'm putting on airs, but with everything that's happened, it's as if my own passions have long since expired."

Momoko lifted her hands from her lap and rested them on her abdomen.

The River's Edge

I

"It's the small trifles that bring us comfort, because it's the small trifles that bring us pain."

Momoko repeated this phrase over and over.

She was trying to convince herself that she could view everything as just another small trifle.

Wasn't it just a small trifle that the Takemiya boy had died?

And wasn't the fact that she hadn't been able to carry his child to term just another small trifle too?

She was only alive today because her stepmother, Asako's birth mother, had swapped her cyanide with sugar. That was all. What was that, if not a small trifle?

When, in the throes of severe illness, she had sensed death's approach, it had felt as though she were being reprimanded. She realized then that everything that had seemed so important to her hadn't mattered at all.

She knew this also: severe illness wasn't limited to ailments of the body but included afflictions of the soul too.

Momoko often experienced such severe illness. Even now, her soul ached. Had it not been that way ever since her birth mother had died, worsening with the death of her lover Keita?

It isn't only human words that can be interpreted at will but divine ones too. Whenever misfortune strikes, there are always convenient words to be found at hand, words of explanation, words of vindication.

But only through keenly felt experience could such words take on a keenly felt reality.

After sleeping with her for the first time, Keita had pushed her away. "What was that? You're pathetic. Truly pathetic."

When she told the Takemiya boy that she was carrying his child, he had protested, he had fled. "It isn't mine. *I'm* the child."

Only she, who had been on the receiving end of those words, could understand their true horror.

Now, they were both dead. As though their own words had come back to punish them. As though those words had been for them both a death sentence.

Keita had died during the war, the Takemiya boy by his own hand.

Three dead, counting the unborn child that she had carried in her womb.

"But if Keita's death in the war wasn't my fault, maybe Little Miya's death wasn't my fault either?" Momoko murmured to herself.

"When Keita died, I tried to kill myself. It wasn't my fault all I swallowed was a capsule of sugar. And I was willing to let Little Miya kill me before he died. It wasn't my fault he loosened his grip around my neck."

But no matter who was responsible, it was an undeniable fact that three lives had been snuffed out.

Hers, however, endured.

"You aren't meant to die," she repeated to herself, straining her ears in the hope of catching an echo of those words.

You aren't meant to die; you are the love of my life, the wife of my heart.

So wrote the poet Ikuta Shungetsu before he threw himself into the waters of the Seto Inland Sea.

"You aren't meant to die."

After the Takemiya boy's death, Momoko found herself imagining that he had said something like that to Asako.

"I'd like her to keep on living once I'm gone."

When she heard those words, Momoko had rebuked Takemiya, had asked if he had come to kill her. Now that he was gone, they echoed in her heart all the louder.

And as they resounded, they brought her back to the suicide of her birth mother, so long ago.

In the cold world that had embraced her mother's suicide, Momoko felt neither guilt nor remorse for the deaths of Keita and Takemiya. Only flames of resentment directed at her father burned inside her.

But the two men had departed this world just as she had surrendered her body to the springtime of youth.

Neither had died a natural death. They had perished violently, before their time. What was she to make of that?

Moreover, she hadn't been able to fully give herself to either before the end. What was she to make of *that*?

The world had been different when she was Asako's age. Maybe her sister, though no older now than Momoko had been back then, having perhaps read such modern books as *The Ideal Marriage* and *Lady Chatterley's Lover,* would be able to understand how she felt?

Momoko had only learned of the Takemiya boy's suicide from Asako's letter.

It was a simple message, but one into which her sister had poured great care and emotion.

The Takemiya boy had died on a mountain in Hakone.

Momoko was sure that he had chosen a place that reminded him of her.

She had taken him there in early spring to enjoy Lake Ashi, and again at the beginning of summer to visit Gōra. He must have chosen one of those two places to end his life, but Asako's letter didn't specify which.

The boy had left no will, no diary, no message of any kind.

Maybe he had written something but destroyed it before the end. Or maybe he hadn't left anything, just as he hadn't penned her a farewell message. Now that she thought about it, he hadn't been the kind of person who kept a diary.

Nor, she realized, had she ever sent him so much as a single postcard. It truly was uncanny.

Perhaps what existed between the two of them had been just as strange.

It did indeed seem like him not to have left behind any written proof of his life.

That description made him seem so fleeting, so faint; but more than that, it seemed to purify, to enrich, to confirm his afterlife.

Momoko knew that the words left by those approaching

death were often no more than deceit, than ostentation, than deluded attempts to adorn oneself in an imaginary reality.

All life, both animal and plant, was destined to perish without leaving lasting words. Just like the stones and water.

Nor had she written a final letter before swallowing the contents of her sugar-filled cyanide capsule.

"You didn't say anything, Little Miya," she said as she read Asako's letter before putting her hands together and breaking down into tears.

"You've no doubt left your family even more desperate to know more. But this is enough for me. Thank you, Little Miya."

In her letter, Asako had advised her not to return to Tōkyō for the time being.

"Such a thoughtful young lady. Thank you for the warning. *You* could never kill anyone, could you?"

Her sister wrote that she had gone to visit Takemiya's grave.

"Why? In my place? To apologize for my sins?"

He had apparently been laid to rest under an old ancestral tombstone, completely at odds with the beautiful youth that he had been.

He was inside her body. He was touching her skin. He was wrapping his arm around her neck. He wasn't in that cemetery. No, he wasn't anywhere anymore.

But all at once, Momoko found herself shivering in fear.

Might not Takemiya have died at the same moment that his child had left her womb?

Asako hadn't mentioned when he had killed himself.

But Momoko felt as though she had been struck by lightning.

"It *must* have happened at the same time. I'm sure of it."

At the exact same moment, she had shed blood, and a life had gone out.

By some mysterious coincidence, a child, so small that there had been no telling whether it had been a boy or a girl, and its father, the one in Kyōto, the other in Hakone, had been called to death at the same instant.

If there really was a road to the afterlife, might not that young, girl-like father be wandering there, holding in his arms a bloodied, still formless child?

"*I'm* still a child," he would murmur . . .

It was true that Momoko herself had made light of him, had treated him as less than an adult, had let down her guard. She hadn't even dreamed of wanting a child from him.

The Takemiya boy was far from her image of an ideal father.

As though struck by a sacred whip, she marveled at the natural vitality, the divine providence that had turned a boy like him into a parent.

But she had decided to give birth to the child. Of course, she hadn't intended to count on him to be a father. It would have been her child, hers alone. And she had resolved to leave her own father's home.

She had hesitated over revealing her pregnancy to Takemiya, but she knew that she wouldn't be able to keep it a secret forever. It was a stroke of fateful irony that she herself had only realized that she was carrying his child after deciding to part ways with him.

When she confessed the truth, while he had been tightening his grip around her neck, she had felt a sudden tenderness for the father of her child.

She had known from the beginning that the news would come to him as a shock, that he would be unlikely to accept the truth of her words.

But he hadn't doubted himself in the least. He hadn't given the possibility that it might be true more than a passing thought. "It isn't mine. You can't fool me."

Of course he hadn't believed her. She had offered nothing in the way of proof. She had been with several others before him. Maybe, like her previous lover, the Nishida boy, he had come to think of her as a temptress. Perhaps it was only natural that he doubted her, that he had considered her a child like him, albeit a more mature one.

After realizing that she was pregnant, Momoko, who had always felt a sense of superiority over him, felt as though their positions had been reversed, as though he was the one looking down on her.

She understood the weakness of womanhood. She couldn't stand it.

It was no different from when she had first slept with Keita, only for him to cast her aside. She couldn't help but wonder whether it wasn't her fate to always be mercilessly humiliated at the hands of men.

Takemiya had fled in the typical, hateful, selfish manner of a man. The child had remained inside her, a woman.

Was her inability to give birth to the child perhaps the female defensive system at work, retaliating against Takemiya as a man?

She had received Asako's letter while still in the hospital.

But Takemiya hadn't fled without a trace. He had killed himself. Or perhaps he *had* fled, through his own death. He had left that mystery for her to solve.

Might he not have chosen death to escape the torment of his suspicion, of his doubt that the child could actually be his?

Perhaps it was a twisted sense of modesty that had led him to declare with such assurance that the child didn't belong to him? Perhaps he hadn't truly doubted her? Might not he have erased his life out of shock and fear at the thought of becoming a father?

"The child is yours, yours alone! I'm just a phantom, a ghost!"

Might not he have spoken those words as he passed from this world?

Momoko herself couldn't think of Takemiya as the father of her child. Her pregnancy seemed rather as a miracle, a blessing bestowed on her alone, as upon the Virgin Mary.

The notion of becoming a mother had struck her as an unexpected wonder.

Even amid the confusion and embarrassment of her unplanned pregnancy, she had felt the sacred bourgeoning of motherhood inside her heart. That was why the Takemiya boy's words at her Kyōto inn had struck her with singular violence.

It was through the offices of Keita's father, Aoki, that she had been admitted to the hospital.

"Are you feeling unwell, Momoko? You look exhausted. I'll feel like I have myself to blame if you fall ill here in Kyōto. I know a doctor, an old friend of mine. I'll call him at once. Let him look you over," he had said casually.

Mizuhara nodded in agreement. "That's a good idea. You can't be too careful. Even Asako, always so fit and healthy, came down with pleurisy."

With the doctor in tow, Aoki came to visit her at her inn and made her promise to let herself be admitted to the hospital the following day. She hadn't been able to resist.

The doctor said that he wanted to take a closer look at her lungs and kidneys and recommended that she be admitted for three or four days for closer examination on account of mental fatigue. He didn't mention her pregnancy. Nonetheless, with the wisdom of experience, he discreetly imparted to her that her condition posed a risk to her body and health.

Momoko understood that this had all been orchestrated between Keita's father and her own, but she let herself go along with their plan. She recognized from the beginning that the examinations were no more than mere pretext.

Neither Aoki nor her father breathed a word about her pregnancy or of the operation. Both men, she knew, were familiar with the vicissitudes of the world. To her relief, they feigned total ignorance. Nor did they call on her by telephone the day before or after.

The matter was buried under a shroud of darkness.

Only now did she realize that she was still a child, that she couldn't possibly hold her own among those adults. If she had been her usual self, she would have rebelled fiercely against their scheme, but now, she was utterly exhausted. After losing the child, she felt only empty inside.

If nothing else, the doctor had no doubt been right when he had diagnosed her with mental exhaustion.

The futon bedding and the kimono that she used while in the hospital were borrowed from the Aoki residence.

"No one has used them in so long. They belonged to my wife. I know you asked for something lively, so I'm sorry these old things are so sober. But I do think these classical motifs take on a certain beauty when worn by a modern young lady like yourself," Aoki had said.

Momoko couldn't understand why he harbored such sympathy and warmth for his late son's former lover, who carried the unborn child of another man, himself no more than a boy.

She understood, however, that while she had tried to keep her pregnancy a secret, he and her father had known all along, had consulted about it behind her back. She felt ashamed in his presence.

Somehow, a tender feminine modesty had taken root inside her and remained even now that the child was gone.

2

Mizuhara put off his return to Tōkyō.

His reasoning, Momoko suspected, had more to do with Takemiya's suicide than her own hospitalization.

With the boy's death, she had begun to regret letting go of the child.

What was she to make of this irreparable sadness?

Her monstrous suspicion that the death of the child that had dwelled within her might have led to the death of its father hung around her neck like a mark of punishment.

The boy, who had obsessively implored her not to cast him aside, was now beyond abandoning.

Whether Takemiya had killed himself out of love for her or out of hatred, whether or not to an outside observer it might have looked as though she had been toying with him for her own amusement, now she, whose life endured, had no choice but to bear all responsibility.

Takemiya had become like Keita, like her late mother. The dead knew no wounds; these injuries of the heart existed only for the living.

Her stay at the hospital had originally been meant to last only three or four days. Nonetheless, her condition took a sudden turn for the worse, alarming her doctors. Her initial diagnosis of mental fatigue had become a reality, the stress that had supported her all this time having now given way.

Her father telephoned her at the hospital, informing her that he wanted to call on her as he was planning to return to Tōkyō in two days' time.

"Don't. Please, don't come," Momoko repeated.

"No? But I won't be able to go home without seeing you. I'm worried."

"There's no need. I don't want to see you right now. I just want to be left alone. You understand, don't you? I'm sorry, Father."

"Oh? I'll be back to take you home, and if I can't because of work, I'll send Asako instead. How does that sound?"

"Asako? Don't send Asako. I can make my way home by myself."

"I know you can. All right, all right. I don't want to torment you about this any further."

"It's fine. I'm more than capable of tormenting myself."

"That isn't what I . . . It's too hard talking over the telephone. I'll come see you."

"I said no. I'm my mother's child, after all."

Her father, undoubtedly shocked, fell silent on the other end of the receiver.

"Hello? I don't want to see you now. I would end up saying something awful again, and then I would hate myself even more."

That was enough to persuade him.

The day after Mizuhara set off back to Tōkyō, Keita's father came to visit her at the hospital.

As she hadn't had time to put on any makeup, Momoko's lips were pale. Her cheeks were sullen.

Nonetheless, Aoki flashed her a bright smile the moment that he entered her room. "How are you feeling? Your sister sent you a letter, so I thought I might come drop it off." He handed her an envelope with his pudgy hands.

"Thank you."

"Your father went back to Tōkyō yesterday. I saw him off at the station. He asked me to take care of you during his absence. I said you would be the one taking care of me."

"Oh?" Momoko replied as though this news was of no concern to her.

"I spoke to your doctor, by the way. He says you should be well enough to leave whenever you feel up to it."

"Did he?" She glanced at Aoki's face before hanging her head once again. "I thought so too."

"That's great." He nodded. "In that case, please, stay as my guest. At least until your father returns to Kyōto."

"Thank you."

Momoko still couldn't tell whether the two men were honestly concerned for her or whether they were simply intent on avoiding a scandal. Until now, she had lived her life however she pleased; but since coming here, after letting herself be steered by them so expertly, the depths of her heart were seething with such anger that she wanted to scream out loud.

"It won't be long before the first frosts. Kyōto is beautiful in late autumn, at the turning of the seasons. But the city is just as famous for its winters. A lot of people here say they actually prefer the winters." Aoki paused before adding in a confidential tone, "Stay and admire the snow. Please."

"When I get out of here, I want to go to the hills of Nishi-yama at least once. I've been watching the sunset over them from my window for days."

"There's a beautiful sunset today as well, don't you think?" Aoki said. "How about we go from Arashiyama to Saga? Most people think of cherry blossoms or autumn leaves when they think of Arashiyama, but I prefer the winters there, when there are no crowds. I went up there by myself, earlier this year. It must have been back in May. I started behind the Tenryūji Temple, climbed to Kameyama Park, and then walked along the ridge of Mount Ogura until I came out at Kita-Saga. That might be a bit much for you right now, though."

Momoko straightened the neckline of her padded kimono. Both it and the haori jacket draped over her shoulders had belonged to Aoki's wife when she was young. The same went for the futon mattress that she was using as a sickbed.

Seeing as these things had all belonged to Keita's mother, Momoko found herself unable to meet Aoki's eyes.

"I'll be going, then." Aoki stood up from his chair. "Is there anything I can get you?"

At that moment, Momoko called after him, "Mr. Aoki. Did my father tell you? That I have another sister here in Kyōto?"

"He did." He turned around to face her. "I met her elder sister."

"She's a geisha, isn't she?"

"That's right."

"Something tells me Asako's letter is about her, our Kyōto sister," Momoko murmured, hesitating. "Could you introduce me to her?"

"Oh? Me? I see. All right. I'll talk to her and see if she won't meet you."

Only after Aoki left did Momoko read Asako's letter. It didn't say anything about their Kyōto sister. In fact, Asako seemed unaware that she had even been hospitalized.

Their father must have returned home by now, but Momoko doubted that he had said anything about her to Asako.

Momoko left the hospital to move into Aoki's house, along with the quilt, washbowl, and other items that she had borrowed.

A few days later, she went with him to Arashiyama. They stepped out of the car at the Togetsukyō Bridge.

"I made a reservation at a restaurant, the Cuckoo, for dinner, but it's still a little early. Why don't we take a walk along the riverbank on the far side?" Aoki glanced toward her.

Momoko nodded. "I remember eating some delicious bamboo sprouts around here when I was little. I wonder if those were from the same restaurant?"

"No doubt." Aoki addressed her again as they crossed the bridge. "I saw a movie while you were in the hospital. Something called *Four Freedoms*. It left me with a strange impression. It was a war documentary about America's struggle and victory over Germany and Italy for what they call their four freedoms. In the end, Hitler and Mussolini, the two dictators, died together with their lovers. They didn't show Hitler's body, seeing as he committed suicide in his bunker beneath his official residence. But Mussolini was caught trying to flee to Switzerland and killed en route. The film showed his corpse, and that of his mistress too. Mussolini, with his huge chin, was hanging there with his eyes wide open. It looked like his body had already started to decay. They were both strung up, hanging from their feet. His mistress's dress was dangling upside down too, bundled up around her chest with her stomach visible for all to see."

The Rainbow Road

I

Keita's father was both horrified and fascinated by the fact that those two dictators had each died alongside their young lovers.

"I could hardly bring myself to look when I saw it. The film started by showing you the stomach of Mussolini's lover. They had hung her from her feet, and her skirt had slipped down. I found myself wondering just how far it was dangling; but thankfully, it was bunched up over her chest, just below her breasts."

Momoko pulled away from Aoki and stopped by the railing of the bridge.

"My apologies," he said, returning to his senses. "It was a vicious spectacle. Rather intolerable, I thought. In two ways. Firstly, because it was so violent and horrible. But also, I sensed in Mussolini's unsightly death more than an attachment *to* life, a sort of radical fulfilment *of* life; something utterly intolerable for us Japanese. It was quite a revelation."

He seemed reluctant to abandon the topic. "It was the kind of thing that we, building our tearooms or admiring the hills of Arashiyama in winter, will never be able to understand."

"But no one else has come to see Arashiyama at this time of year."

Apart from Momoko and Aoki, there were no other figures crossing the Togetsukyō Bridge.

"It's a shame. Arashiyama is beautiful, even after the autumn colors have faded."

"Yes. There's a stillness, a sense of melancholy." Momoko stared down into the river. "The pine trees are a lovely color. Their green leaves almost look like they're a glistening shade of blue."

The left bank of the river was lined with pine trees, while a sparse grove stretched out on the right. Glancing around, Momoko saw that the slopes of Mount Arashiyama beyond the bridge, along with Mount Kameyama and Mount Ogura farther out, were likewise clad in pines.

Plumes of smoke from two bonfires arose from a small island at the lower reaches of the river.

Silhouetted behind that smoke was the outline of the hills of Higashiyama.

"Up to the bridge here, it's called the Ōi River, meaning *great barrier,* but it's called the Katsura River from this point onward. True to its name, the water is dammed up, forming a basin of sorts in front of Mount Arashiyama. Farther upstream, it has a different name again, the Hozu River." Aoki continued walking, all but urging Momoko to follow.

"Did you ever conduct the coming-of-age pilgrimage to a temple when you were thirteen?" he asked her.

"No."

"It's a tradition here in the Kansai region. The Hōrinji Temple holds it every year on the thirteenth of April. The cherry trees are in full bloom, and there are always so many people milling in front of the statue of the bodhisattva Ākāśagarbha."

On the other side of the bridge, the multistoried pagoda of the Hōrinji stood out like a fresh coat of color.

Aoki began to describe the Festival of the Boats, a celebration held in verdant spring in imitation of the pleasures enjoyed by ancient nobles, featuring poetry, songs, and music. During the autumn colors, those boats were joined by other period-decorated vessels from the Tenryūji, and another named after the merchant Suminokura Ryōi.

But it was difficult in winter to imagine the gaiety of those festivities. Now, the dammed river formed a deep, silent basin, filled with dark winter hues.

"How about we take a short walk?" After crossing the Togetsukyō Bridge, Aoki turned right along the riverbank.

The path led up toward Mount Arashiyama, but it too was deserted. The water that they had seen from atop the bridge now flowed but a short distance away.

"You can see the rocks at the bottom of the river," Momoko said, pausing to look. "Yet the water looks so deep."

The rocks, clearly visible through the depths of the water, seemed somehow mystical. A school of small fish was swimming above them.

"Aren't you cold?" Aoki asked. "You've just come out of the hospital, after all."

"No. When you came to see me the other day, when you told me I could leave whenever I wanted, I suddenly felt much better."

"It wasn't *me* who said that. It was the doctor."

"Oh? Maybe I've been relying on others too much?"

"Do you think so? I would say the opposite. From my standpoint, it looks to me like you're far too tough on yourself."

"No." Momoko shook her head.

"It's true." Aoki smiled. "Well, putting your case aside for a moment, when people see someone who is already tormenting themselves, they're sometimes drawn to add to that torment. You can substitute the word *fate* for *people,* if you prefer. I suppose it does sound rather vulgar to mix and match those two words, but trying to separate our individual fate from the people and the world around us leads only to loneliness and solitude."

"Oh?" Momoko didn't know how to respond. "Did you make that speech to my father too?"

"We spoke a little about it."

"But I don't torment myself. No, there was a time when I thought that was true, but I don't know anymore."

"You don't like to rely on others, do you?"

Momoko felt her face turning red, burning with embarrassment. "On others? You've all done so much for me, but I'm too ashamed to offer my thanks."

"I didn't want to bring this up now, but if you go back to Tōkyō like this, I worry you'll end up taking that mental baggage of yours back with you, your habit of tormenting yourself. You might end up resenting yourself for having gone along with what your father and I planned."

"I *do* resent myself. I'm ashamed . . ." Her voice trailed off.

"You should let others carry that burden."

Momoko couldn't answer.

But hadn't she already pushed it on others?

Now, rather than remorse, it was profound shame that lingered inside her.

If Aoki and her father had played a cunning trick on her, wasn't she more cunning still for having knowingly gone along with it? Her heart smoldered with a grievous sense of self-loathing for the guile to which, in her desperation, she had consigned herself.

Her father and Aoki, but most of all she herself, were acting as though nothing at all had happened.

The fact that she had allowed Aoki to drag her so meekly to Arashiyama seemed to her a continuation of that feigned indifference.

No woman concerned about her modesty would have agreed to stay at Aoki's home after being discharged from the hospital. She had surrendered herself, had left everything in the hands of others.

She understood that he was asking her to trust him, to let him handle it all.

She saw plainly how docile she had become to the will of others, unable to offer even token resistance. Her heart was empty. In a way, she even found Aoki's compassion soothing, and so held tightly to him. But at the same time, his presence was oppressive, like an overcast sky.

"Keita shouldn't have gone off to die," he said. "The dead are easily forgiven. Because it's impossible to chase after them, to reach them, to punish them in any way. It may be a profound truth for those of us who are alive today, who will one day die, that the dead escape condemnation. But it's fine to put the blame on them. That's what I think."

"But . . ." Momoko began, before falling silent.

Did Keita's father know, perhaps, what his son had done to her?

"My mother ended her own life too. You must have heard from my father."

"I know. So let's lay those sins on Keita and your mother."

"What sins?" Momoko asked outright.

"All of them. The sufferings of the living."

"Do you mean to plunge them into hell?"

"Do you *want* to send Keita to hell?"

"No." Momoko shook her head.

"You can try so hard not to push your loved ones into hell that you end up falling into it yourself. Sometimes, I find myself thinking that none of our pains, none of our sins, are wholly original. They're an inheritance, imitations of those who preceded us. Our traditions and customs are all inherited from the dead, don't you think?"

"Maybe we would be better off as birds? Building identical nests for thousands and thousands of years?"

"Little birds don't have architects like your father." Aoki laughed. "Anyway, let's agree that the fault rests with the dead. I know I apologized to you on Keita's behalf, but I've come to believe it isn't the responsibility of the living to erase the sins of the dead. Rather, we should think more about giving thanks to each other. At least that's how it seems to me."

"Is that why you're so considerate toward me?"

"Let's call it that." Aoki lowered his voice. "Whenever we meet, I always end up mentioning Keita, and that alone makes me want to do whatever I can to help. I would love for you to come snow viewing here in Kyōto with me, and to usher in the new year together. I invited your father to visit on New Year's Eve, even if only for one night. He did mention how he wanted to hear the ringing of the temple bells in person for once, rather than just over the radio."

"I'll try to make a fresh start with him too," Momoko said offhandedly.

In truth, she was amazed that her father could have returned home while entrusting her to Aoki. Had that been, perhaps, an act of cowardice?

Or had her father left her here in Kyōto so that Asako wouldn't learn of her pregnancy?

Momoko felt as though she had no home to which to return.

"I might still have Natsuji, but he's his own man. He can't replace Keita." Aoki, it seemed, was still reminiscing over his lost son.

The reflection of a small tree on the riverbank caught Momoko's eye. It was a web of fine branches, drawn clearly over the water. What kind of tree was it? Above the embankment, its intricate, delicate lines were difficult to distinguish among the surrounding foliage, yet they stood out perfectly on the surface of the river. It was as though she were staring not at a reflection but at a tree growing *inside* the water. It was just an ordinary tree, and yet it stirred in her such a ghostly feeling.

She was mesmerized by what she saw. "I could never imagine such clear blue water in Tōkyō."

She looked up and found that the hill opposite was reflected in the water too. The trunks of its many pines were more vivid in hue reflected on the river than they were in the world above.

The earthen walls of the Rinsenji Temple at the foot of the mountains were visible at the base of the pine trees.

"It's a perfect winter landscape," Aoki said, staring back at the hill reflected in the water.

"I heard it hailed in Tōkyō the other day. My sister mentioned it in her letter. And there was a rainbow after it stopped hailing. I don't know exactly where she was, but she was walking along a wide road when a rainbow stretched down in front of her. She said she walked straight toward the middle of it."

Momoko had gotten the sense while reading the letter that Asako and Natsuji had journeyed toward the rainbow in each other's company. Indeed, she felt the same way now.

Yet she didn't tell Natsuji's father that.

Now she was walking alongside Keita's father, Natsuji's father, through a secluded path in Arashiyama; or rather, she found herself reflecting on the chain of events that had brought her here.

The steep stone walls and rock formations of the upper course of the river slowly came into view, enclosed on either side by Mount Arashiyama and Mount Kameyama.

She came to a stop as the path rose into the shade of the trees.

"Shall we turn back?" Aoki asked.

"Yes."

On the far shore, someone was burning a pile of dry leaves. A cotton flag was waving nearby.

"That's the Cuckoo. I invited your Kyōto sister to meet us there, after you said you wanted to see her."

"Oh? She's there now?" Momoko asked sternly. "Why didn't you say something? How awful, trying to catch me off guard like that."

"I'm sorry. I wanted it to be a surprise, but I've ended up giving it away ahead of time."

"You adults are truly incorrigible."

"Yes, but it isn't a sure thing she'll even come. I spoke to her elder sister shortly after noon, but she couldn't give me a definite answer."

Momoko held her silence, walking on ahead.

Evening clouds had appeared over Mount Hiei, and the Higashiyama area was shrouded in mist. A thin fog had begun to seep down from the trees of Mount Ogura nearby.

2

"Oh?" Momoko said aloud, startling the moment that she was shown into the private dining room at the Cuckoo.

So the girl whom she had met at the Miyako Odori had been her sister?

Wakako stared at her sternly.

"Have you met before?" Aoki asked.

"Yes. But I didn't know at the time."

Wakako and her mother bowed their heads before Momoko could take her seat.

"Welcome. This is Wakako," the older woman said, motioning toward the younger. "And I'm Kikue."

"Mizuhara Momoko."

Kikue bowed her head again. "On this occasion, I . . . I'm afraid I'm at a loss for words."

Aoki moved to fill the uneasy silence, turning to Momoko. "Actually, this is my first time meeting you all as well."

"You've been so kind, truly . . . I don't know what I can possibly do to thank you."

"We've met before, so there's no need, really." Momoko paused before asking, "You realized who we were when we met at the theater, didn't you, Wakako?"

"Yes."

"How?"

"The business card you gave Mr. Ōtani."

"Ah, the child's father?"

"Yes."

"And you ran away as soon as you guessed who we were?"

"She didn't run away," Kikue said, turning to her daughter in embarrassment. "She was in shock, weren't you?"

"It's fine, really. It doesn't matter. I would probably have done the same thing in her position."

"No, miss, you wouldn't have run away. If you had been in Wakako's place, your heart would have been broken. Even today, she said she was so ashamed she didn't want to come here. I'm even more mortified, seeing as she didn't have the heart to come alone."

"Did you know I wasn't born in our father's house either?" Momoko asked frankly.

Kikue, sensing at once that she was referring to the fact that she wasn't the daughter of her father's lawful wife, lowered her gaze. "And yet you *were* raised in that house, miss."

"Because my mother was dead."

"Don't say that. Should I have died too?"

"I wonder. Why don't we ask Wakako?" Momoko pushed back lightly. "Which would have made you happier?"

"Which indeed?" Kikue responded. "Happiness is a difficult thing. Even if it meant its own sorrows, maybe she would have found it preferable."

"I wonder. If Wakako was to come live with us . . ."

"Out of the question! How could you even consider such a thing?"

Kikue was flustered, dismayed by the suggestion. Mizuhara had suggested the same thing that spring, but to hear it broached once more . . .

Nonetheless, she decided against revealing their encounter at the Daitokuji.

"Please don't trouble yourself over her. She's her mother's child."

"It's my sister Asako who keeps dwelling on it. She visited Kyōto alone at the end of last year looking for you."

"Oh." Kikue had already heard this from Mizuhara and had informed Wakako too.

"I told her it was for the best she didn't find you. That we all had our own separate lives." Momoko glanced at her other sister. "Now that we've met each other, do you feel a sisterly bond between us, Wakako?"

Wakako blushed, her head still bowed.

Her lashes and eyebrows were thin and delicate, her eyes light brown in hue, though her hair seemed somehow wispy. Momoko realized that she had said something cruel.

"This isn't your first meeting," Kikue remarked.

With that prompt, Wakako spoke up. "I realized you were my sister when we met at the theater six months ago. I've held that image in my heart ever since. I've dreamed about calling you my sisters."

"Please do. For Asako's sake, at least. She would have been so happy if she had known the truth back then. You saw how much she doted on the baby you were helping look after."

"Yes. Mr. Ōtani was moved too," Wakako said.

"I think Asako was moved by him." Momoko laughed.

"Mr. Ōtani was indeed impressed," Kikue said. "And Wakako's eyes were positively sparkling after she came back from the theater that day. She kept on telling me what sweet, beautiful young ladies her sisters were. She couldn't even sleep that night. I said she was lucky to meet you. I really did think it was for the best. Of course, she doesn't have the same social standing you both do, and she'll have to find her own way to ford the river of life. But when she encounters pain and hardship, the thought of her sisters in Tōkyō should bring her some consolation. I can't speak for her feelings, but I suppose they must be similar to mine on that count. Mr. Mizuhara and I . . . well, he left me a long time ago, but it was my reverence for him that helped me to ford these currents by myself." Kikue was moved to tears. "Wakako doesn't need to join her Tōkyō sisters, or confide in them. It's enough just to know they're kind and beautiful."

Momoko had difficulty deciding her next words. "Has she met Father recently?"

"Not since she was little. Maybe twelve or thirteen years ago."

"Oh?"

"We went to admire the camellias at the Daitokuji. You weren't old enough to walk yet," Kikue said, turning to her daughter.

"I don't remember."

"You should meet our father," Momoko declared.

Kikue bowed her head. "Thank you for saying that, but we don't want to bother him. Now that we've had the pleasure of meeting you, we'll wait for him to call on us. We can't have you embarrass yourself, Wakako."

Momoko remained silent.

Kikue, remembering how her daughter's eyes had filled with tears when she had seen her off on her way to meet her father at the Daitokuji, found her own eyes growing moist.

Aoki called the maid over and asked her to bring out the meal.

"How about a toast between sisters?" he suggested.

"Yes," Momoko agreed reluctantly. "But how strange. Three sisters, each born to different mothers."

Nonetheless, she took her cup in her hands and glanced up at Wakako, urging her to do likewise.

Her sister, however, didn't move.

"What's wrong? Have I offended you?"

Wakako shook her head, but still she didn't reach for her cup.

Kikue watched on without prevailing on her daughter. "Living in a neighborhood of geisha, perhaps she doesn't like toasts?"

"Oh? Then let's dispense with the theatrics," Momoko said, setting her own cup down.

Kikue had come out with a clever excuse, but Momoko doubted that Wakako truly felt that way.

In any case, her sister's refusal to accept the cup had struck her as deeply pure and fervent.

"I suppose we should wait until Father can see us both,"

Momoko said, rising to her feet. "The sun must be setting over Mount Arashiyama around now."

She slid open the shōji screen.

From beyond the winter-stripped trees, she could make out the soft murmur of the river.